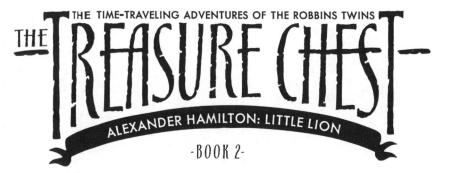

THE TIME-TRAVELING ADVENTURES OF THE ROBBINS TWINS

THE TREASURE CHEST

ALEXANDER HAMILTON: LITTLE LION

-BOOK 2-

BY *NEW YORK TIMES* BEST-SELLING AUTHOR

ANN HOOD

Grosset & Dunlap
An Imprint of Penguin Group (USA) Inc.

Hochhauser

GROSSET & DUNLAP
Published by the Penguin Group
Penguin Group (USA) Inc., 375 Hudson Street, New York, New York 10014, USA
Penguin Group (Canada), 90 Eglinton Avenue East, Suite 700, Toronto, Ontario M4P 2Y3, Canada
(a division of Pearson Penguin Canada Inc.)
Penguin Books Ltd, 80 Strand, London WC2R 0RL, England
Penguin Ireland, 25 St Stephen's Green, Dublin 2, Ireland
(a division of Penguin Books Ltd)
Penguin Group (Australia), 707 Collins Street, Melbourne, Victoria 3008, Australia
(a division of Pearson Australia Group Pty Ltd)
Penguin Books India Pvt Ltd, 11 Community Centre, Panchsheel Park, New Delhi—110 017, India
Penguin Group (NZ), 67 Apollo Drive, Rosedale, Auckland 0632, New Zealand
(a division of Pearson New Zealand Ltd)
Penguin Books (South Africa), Rosebank Office Park, 181 Jan Smuts Avenue, Parktown North 2193, South Africa
Penguin China, B7 Jiaming Center, 27 East Third Ring Road North, Chaoyang District, Beijing 100020, China

Penguin Books Ltd, Registered Offices: 80 Strand, London WC2R 0RL, England

Text © 2012, 2013 by Ann Hood. Art © 2013 by Denis Zilber. Published by Grosset & Dunlap, a division of Penguin Young Readers Group, 345 Hudson Street, New York, New York 10014. GROSSET & DUNLAP is a trademark of Penguin Group (USA) Inc. Printed in the U.S.A.

Library of Congress Control Number: 2011008928

Design by Giuseppe Castellano.
Map illustration by Giuseppe Castellano and © 2013 by Penguin Group (USA) Inc.

ISBN 978-0-448-45468-9 (pbk)   10 9 8 7 6 5 4 3 2 1
ISBN 978-0-448-45472-6 (hc)   10 9 8 7 6 5 4 3 2 1

ALWAYS LEARNING   PEARSON

For Francesco Sedita

CHAPTER 1

The Holland Tunnel

October arrived in Newport, Rhode Island, with bright blue skies, puffy white clouds, and perfect cool autumn temperatures. The leaves on the trees along Bellevue Avenue began to turn red and gold and orange, and the tourists who clogged the streets all summer were gone, taking with them the traffic and crowds. For most children, October in Newport was idyllic. But not for Maisie and Felix Robbins. They wanted to be back in New York City, in their apartment at 10 Bethune Street, with their parents still married and their lives the way they had been before the divorce six months earlier had changed everything.

That was why early on that beautiful October

morning, when other children were down the road playing softball or out on the bay sailing or with their families buying apples and pumpkins in nearby Tiverton, Maisie and Felix sneaked down the stairs of the small third-floor apartment where they lived and into Elm Medona, the mansion their great-great-grandfather Phinneas Pickworth had built over a hundred years ago. Elm Medona technically belonged to the local preservation society now, but family members could still live in the apartment. The mansion had a room called The Treasure Chest, and in that room, stacked and nestled and leaning against one another, were artifacts and curiosities of all kinds: feathers, seashells, rocks; wands and sticks and canes; pieces of glass and string and paper; sealing wax, fountain pens, scales, compasses, tarnished silverware, dried watercolors, maps. The items in The Treasure Chest appeared to be limitless. Everywhere Maisie and Felix looked, they found yet another thing that caught their attention.

A few weeks earlier, they had gone into The Treasure Chest and found a letter with a list of names on it. Somehow, that letter brought them back in time to Clara Barton's farm in Oxford,

Massachusetts, in 1836. Even though they had spent the night there, when they returned it seemed like no time had passed at all. Although they weren't sure how they actually time traveled—or how they got back—what Maisie and Felix wanted was to do it again. But with a new school and so many new things to think about, they couldn't find the right time to go to The Treasure Chest. And this time they wanted to go back six months and land in their old beds in New York City.

Even though it was a Saturday, their mother had gone to work at the law office. Back in New York, she had spent three years going to NYU law school, giving up her dream of becoming an actress and starring in a Broadway musical. Now she had her chance to prove herself. Fishbaum and Fishbaum was one of the oldest law firms in Newport, and their mother felt lucky to have this job. As a result, she had prepared them that she would work long hours and weekends. She had to.

They waited for her to leave, then met in the hallway between their rooms. The apartment where they lived was the former servants' quarters. But below them lay the enormous Elm Medona, a seventy-room mansion filled with tapestries from the Middle Ages, marble fireplaces imported from France, ceilings trimmed with real gold leaf, and the Pickworth symbols of peonies, peacocks, and pineapples painted and carved and etched into almost everything. The house was so big that when they went there alone at night, their voices echoed and their footsteps seemed to thunder as they walked across the vast marble floors.

Just like the last time, Felix climbed into the dumbwaiter in the kitchen and let Maisie send it down into the mansion's basement. This time, though, he wasn't at all afraid. Instead, he concentrated on their mission. Last night, their father had called from Doha, Qatar, where he'd gone to work at a new art museum, and the sound of his voice had made Felix's chest ache in such a way that he wondered if he might be actually having a heart attack. He didn't think kids had heart attacks, but Felix found himself gasping for air as his chest tightened, all the while his father described the compound where he lived and the camel market and the sand dunes that sung.

When his father hung up, Felix found himself

even more certain that The Treasure Chest had to bring him and Maisie back to their small apartment in New York City, back to where they all belonged. Now, he wrapped his arms around himself like a hug as the dumbwaiter creaked downward. He closed his eyes and imagined their old block with the supermarket on one corner and the diner that his father said had the worst coffee in New York City on the other corner. He pictured the long corridor that led to their apartment, the row of locks that lined their front door, the way the lights in the small foyer came on as soon as someone stepped inside.

Maisie's voice interrupted his concentration. "Are you going to live in the dumbwaiter or something?"

Felix opened his eyes. The dumbwaiter had come to a stop. Out its small window, the white tiled kitchen gleamed at him.

A mantra, Felix decided. He needed a mantra to keep him focused.

"Home," he whispered to himself. *Home.* He repeated it as he pushed open the door and waited for Maisie to join him. *Home. Home.*

"Home?" Maisie said, peering into his face. Like

the last time, she had followed him down in the dumbwaiter. She stood three inches taller than her twin brother and had a way of looking down at Felix that made her seem powerful.

"My mantra," Felix explained.

Maisie considered the idea. "That's good," she said finally. "But do you think we should be more specific? Like repeat our address or something?"

Felix shrugged. "*Home* just feels right," he said.

She grinned at him. "*Home* it is then, little brother."

At seven minutes older, Maisie liked to remind Felix at every opportunity who was born first.

They walked up the stairs and into the Grand Ballroom, both of them whispering *home, home, home* over and over. The early morning sun came through the stained glass window at the landing of the stairs, sending blue and gold light onto the polished marble floor.

"It looks different in daytime," Maisie said, pausing to look up at the window with its peacock pattern.

Felix stopped, too, following her gaze.

"Pretty," she said.

"Phinneas Pickworth commissioned Louis Comfort Tiffany to make this window for Elm Medona," Felix said in a deep voice, reciting the words the Woman in Pink had told them when they'd taken a tour of the mansion. The local preservation society had arranged a VIP tour for them with a special guide, even though Maisie and Felix called her the Woman in Pink because of all the pink she wore. She had led them through every room, giving excruciating details about everything in them. "Notice how his favorite symbols are incorporated in the window. The peacock—"

"The pineapple," Maisie added.

"And the peony," Felix said.

"How posh!" Maisie giggled.

They both laughed and continued across the ballroom to the Grand Staircase, Maisie's arm hooked into Felix's. Halfway up they paused again, this time to look at the black-and-white picture of their Great-Aunt Maisie and her twin brother, Thorne, as children. They had grown up here at Elm Medona. Great-Aunt Maisie had lived in the servants' quarters on the third floor until she'd had her stroke and moved into an assisted living facility.

They both peered at the mischievous-looking boy in the picture with a prominent cowlick and slightly too large ears.

"No one ever mentions him," Maisie said.

Felix shivered inexplicably.

"I wonder—" Maisie began.

But Felix interrupted her. "Remember our mantra?" he said. "If we lose our focus, we could end up who knows where."

"Right," Maisie said.

They continued up the stairs. At the top, Maisie gently ran her hand along the green wall until she felt the spot to gently push. The wall opened and slowly spun to reveal the hidden staircase that led to The Treasure Chest. Even though they had done this very thing before, Felix couldn't help but gasp. *A secret staircase! Hidden behind a door!*

"Should I go up alone, like last time?" Maisie said.

When they'd traveled to the Barton farm in 1836, Maisie and Felix had repeated everything exactly as the first time they'd sneaked inside. That first time they'd realized the power of The Treasure Chest something mysterious and terrifying and thrilling had started to happen: Loud noises and the smell of gunpowder had filled the room, and suddenly Maisie and Felix had found themselves lifting off the ground. But then their mother had arrived home, startling them enough to stay in place. When they tried again a few days later, they'd been careful to repeat everything they'd done and said.

"I don't think so," Felix said. "I think we can both go inside and choose an object and see what happens."

"That seems too easy," Maisie said.

"Well," Felix said thoughtfully, "we'll need to find something that looks like it belongs in New York, I think."

Maisie shook her head. "There must be more to it than that."

"Let's try it this way," Felix said.

"Okay," Maisie said reluctantly.

That decided, they climbed the secret staircase and went directly to The Treasure Chest. Maisie unclipped the red velvet rope that kept the room off-limits, and they both stepped inside.

"Smells like the Museum of Natural History in here," Maisie said, sniffing. "I didn't notice that last time."

Felix glanced around the room, trying to take it

all in. "So much old stuff," he said. "It's kind of like a museum."

Maisie picked up a jade box, bringing it close to examine it.

"No!" Felix shouted. "Don't just start picking stuff up! For all we know, that could take us to China. We need to focus."

Maisie replaced the box hesitantly.

"You want us to just close our eyes and say 'home, home, home' and hope it works?" she said, her eyes blazing.

"I don't know. Maybe."

Maisie couldn't help herself. She needed to touch the objects. Her hands lightly skimmed a small gold telescope, a creased map, seedpods, an arrowhead.

"We need to find an object that will help us get back home," she said. "Remember how Clara needed that letter? Somehow we need to pick up something . . . I don't know . . . New Yorky."

"Maybe," Felix said again, even more uncertainly.

Maisie walked slowly around the room. She was sure that somewhere among all these things was the perfect object, the very one that could get them back to Bethune Street.

A drawing caught her eye. Not a regular drawing, but a thin, white paper with lines drawn in faded ink. Maisie picked it up. Immediately, she realized that it was a blueprint for a long structure of some kind. It had two side-by-side tubes and a series of fans and ducts in a pattern along the top.

"Hudson River Vehicular Tunnel," Felix read over her shoulder.

"That's funny," Maisie said. "There is no Hudson River Tunnel. There's the Lincoln Tunnel and the—"

"Put it down!" Felix shouted at her.

Startled, Maisie dropped the blueprints, which fluttered to the floor, landing opened on the Oriental carpet.

"Did you see the name on those?" Felix said, wide-eyed.

Maisie shook her head,

"Clifford Millburn *Holland*," Felix said.

"The Holland Tunnel?" Maisie said. That was the tunnel their family took whenever they left Manhattan and headed south to Cape May, New Jersey, where they sometimes rented a little house near the beach.

Felix pointed to the blueprints. "1920," he said.

Maisie squinted at the signature and the date beneath it. "Wow!" she said, bending to pick it up again.

"Are you crazy?" Felix said. "That will bring us back to 1920."

"Look at all this stuff, Felix," Maisie said, sweeping her arms. "It's all old. No matter what object we pick, it's older than this year. Older than probably this century."

She was right, Felix realized, his heart sinking. Phinneas Pickworth had collected everything in this room. Of course none of it would do them any good.

"But maybe if we can just get back to New York, we can find our way to the time we want," Maisie was saying.

"I don't know," Felix said. "What if we get stuck in the wrong decade? What if that's what happened to Great-Uncle Thorne? What if he went somewhere and never came back?"

"Look, I don't know how we'll do it," Maisie said, smoothing the creases in the blueprint. "I just think we can figure it out. We time traveled, didn't we? And we got back, didn't we?"

"But that was just luck or something."

Maisie remembered their mantra. She looked at that beautiful drawing of the Holland Tunnel, and she thought about all of them, a family, sitting in their parents' beat-up silver Volvo with its broken air-conditioning. Her legs stuck to the seat with sweat and her lips tasted salty. By the time they got through the Holland Tunnel, she and Felix were already asking for snacks and drinks and wanting to know how much longer before they got to Cape May. Maisie always wore her bathing suit under her clothes so that she could get into the ocean that much sooner. Sometimes her father lifted her onto his shoulders and carried her into the water that way. She could feel how slippery his skin was and how tightly his hands gripped her ankles as they made their way forward. She could see the small, quarter-sized bald spot on the top of his head with his pink scalp showing through.

Felix sighed and took hold of the opposite corners of the blueprint. He believed that they both needed to hold the object in order to time travel.

"Home," Felix whispered.

Maisie smiled. "Home," she whispered back.

Nothing happened.

"Maybe tug on it?" she said finally. "Remember we kind of yanked on that letter."

Felix tugged. Then he tugged harder. Something was different. Wrong somehow. The air did not feel electric or special. The room didn't seem to quiver. There was just the musty museum smell and the rough paper in his hands and his sister's shallow breaths.

"I know!" Maisie said brightly. "We were standing over there. Maybe that spot is magical."

Felix followed her to the spot where they'd stood holding the letter for Clara Barton.

"Home," he said softly.

"Home," Maisie repeated.

He closed his eyes and yanked, just like he did before. He held his breath. Then he opened his eyes.

Felix and Maisie had gone exactly nowhere.

CHAPTER 2

The Missing Piece

"Something is wrong!" Maisie said angrily, stomping her foot for effect.

"Maybe it was a one-shot thing," Felix said. As that idea settled in him, he felt almost relieved. "One time travel per lifetime," he added, liking the way that sounded.

True, the thought of returning to their old life had made him eager to do it again. But once Maisie decided she would even risk going back to New York City in 1920 and then figure out what to do from there, Felix's excitement had faded. If he couldn't go back to Bethune Street with his family intact, then he would just make do here in Newport. Maisie, he knew, was not making any new friends. She had the worst teacher in the entire school, and she got in trouble all the time. To her, anything would be better than this.

"Think," Maisie ordered. "What are we doing wrong?"

"Really," Felix said, trying not to sound too eager, "I think we should just go back to the apartment and forget all about it."

She narrowed her eyes at him. "I thought you wanted to go back to New York," she said.

"To *our* New York. Not New York in 1920 when there wasn't even the Holland Tunnel yet."

Maisie still held the blueprints tightly in both hands. She glanced down at them before she said, "The Holland Tunnel is on Canal Street, right? If we got back, we'd be what? Twelve blocks from home?"

"But the timing is off!" Felix said, frustrated. Then a thought occurred to him. "The timing is way off!" he said. "That letter for Clara was dated almost thirty years after we saw her, remember? So if we went back and met Clifford Holland, it could be way before 1920. Maybe even before 1900."

"I didn't think of that," Maisie said, furrowing

her brow in concentration. "The rules of this are so complicated. If we could just figure them out, we could control where we went and when. I'm sure of it."

Felix shook his head. "I think it was a fluke," he said. "That weird storm that blew in during the tour of the mansion. Remember how freaked out the docent got? The vase fixing itself somehow. All of it."

In the middle of their VIP tour, the wind broke a fancy Ming vase into a million pieces. Then, magically, the vase got put back together. Almost. Maisie had managed to keep a shard of it for herself. And mysteriously one other shard remained missing.

Now, Felix started to walk out of The Treasure Chest, and to his surprise, his sister followed him, placing the blueprints back on the desk as she passed it.

"I'm not giving up, you know," Maisie said as she closed the wall back up.

"I know," Felix said.

They began down the Grand Staircase in silence. But at the landing, Maisie paused and looked right in the eyes of young Great-Aunt Maisie's picture.

"What do you know about all this?" Maisie said to the photograph.

As soon as she said it, her face brightened.

"What does Great-Aunt Maisie know?" she said, excited.

Before Felix could answer, Maisie grabbed his arm. "She knows something. If we ask her why it didn't work this time, maybe she can help us."

Uh-oh, Felix thought as Maisie pulled him down the stairs with her. He knew she was right. Great-Aunt Maisie could tell them exactly what to do, and once she did, there would be no stopping his sister.

$

"Why didn't we think about this in the first place?" Maisie said, pleased with herself.

She and Felix stood at a bus stop on Bellevue Avenue, waiting for a bus that would take them to Great-Aunt Maisie's assisted living facility.

"At home, we took the subway by ourselves all the time," she added. "I can't believe I didn't think about taking a bus wherever we want to go."

Across the street stood the Tennis Hall of Fame, and Maisie watched as men in dark red pants and polo shirts went in and out. Normally the way people dressed here bugged her. Grown women wore belts with little whales and ladybugs on them and men wore boat shoes and pants like these guys, which were practically pink. But today, at this minute, instead of bugging her, Maisie was delighted by all of it. Today she felt in charge of her life. She would get on a bus and go to Great-Aunt Maisie and find out . . . well, something. Wasn't that what Clara Barton had suggested? Hadn't Clara herself said that their aunt might have a lot of things to teach them and that they should listen to her?

A bus came down Bellevue Avenue, slowing at the stop. Maisie and Felix climbed on, shoving coins into the turnstile. Even that simple act felt wonderful to Maisie. It was like being in a city again. At the subway stations in New York, she always got a tiny thrill whenever she pushed through the turnstile. She loved looking down the long tracks and seeing the lights of an approaching train. Maisie smiled. She could come to love buses, too, she decided as she slid into a window seat.

They were the only passengers, and Maisie relaxed into the blue seat. Pressing her face against the glass, she stared out at the stores and restaurants they passed. In the distance, she saw Narragansett Bay gleaming in the morning light and a few sailboats with puffed-out sails moving across it. She might like it here, Maisie thought, if their father lived with them, too.

Felix nudged her with his elbow.

Up ahead, the Island Retirement Center came into sight. Maisie reached up and pulled the cord for the bus to stop, and she and Felix made their way down the aisle.

"Thank you," Maisie said to the driver.

"You visiting someone special?" he asked her.

His eyes reminded her of the water she'd been gazing at just a moment ago.

"Our great-aunt," Maisie said.

The driver seemed to be looking right through her with those eyes.

"Maisie, come on!" Felix called from the sidewalk.

"You go on now," the driver said.

Maisie hurried off the bus. She and Felix made their way up the front walk that led to the Island Retirement Center, Maisie walking quickly ahead of him. She couldn't wait to hear what Great-Aunt Maisie might tell them.

$

Great-Aunt Maisie sat in the chintz chair in her room, dressed in a pale blue silk dressing gown with a matching robe. The last time they had visited her, she'd looked pale and old, but today she had on face powder, small spots of rouge on her sharp cheekbones, and her favorite Chanel Red lipstick. Usually, that makeup on her frail face made her look kind of scary, but Maisie thought their great-aunt actually looked pretty sitting there.

When she saw them in the doorway, Great-Aunt Maisie brightened.

"It's about time you two showed up," she said happily.

Maisie and Felix glanced at each other. Ever since she'd had her stroke back in the spring, Great-Aunt Maisie's speech had been so garbled they'd had trouble understanding her. But now her words were clear and clipped, with her slight rich person's accent evident again.

Great-Aunt Maisie pointed to the peach-colored Victorian love seat across from her.

"Please sit down. Perhaps one of these dreadful nurses can even bring us some tea."

She picked up a small silver bell from the round wooden table beside her and gave it a good, hard shake. With her pursed lips and hard-set jaw, Maisie could tell her aunt was not happy at all. Immediately, a nurse appeared.

"Miss Pickworth, that bell has to go. There's a buzzer right there for you to call us," the nurse said as she bustled in. She had on mauve scrubs and purple Crocs, and her hair was in a sloppy bun held up with a big clip.

"That buzzer is uncivilized," Great-Aunt Maisie said. "I've already told you that. I've been calling servants for almost a century, and I always use a bell."

The nurse put her hands on her hips and glared at Great-Aunt Maisie. "I. Am. Not. A. Servant," she said through gritted teeth. "I have a degree from the University of Rhode Island in nursing and—"

"Yes, yes, that's lovely, dear," Great-Aunt Maisie said, fluttering her fingers dismissively. "Now we'd like a nice pot of tea."

She looked at Maisie and Felix, who were stunned by how lively their aunt had become.

"Earl Grey?" she asked them. Before they answered, she returned her gaze to the nurse. "Yes," Great-Aunt Maisie said. "Earl Grey. And some of the shortbread I had delivered."

"Miss Pickworth—" the nurse fumed.

"And please use my sterling teapot, dear. The Pickworths have been drinking their tea from that teapot since the turn of the century." Great-Aunt Maisie paused. "The turn of the last century," she added, pleased with herself.

The nurse took a deep breath. Her cheeks burned bright red.

"Why are you still standing there?" Great-Aunt Maisie asked her.

Frustrated, the nurse turned around and stomped out, her bun slipping out of its clip.

"I must talk to her about her attire," Great-Aunt Maisie said. "No one looks good in all that purple. And her hair needs a trim." She thought a moment, then said, "Perhaps I'll have Henri come and do her hair for her. Yes! That's a wonderful idea."

She picked up a small notebook and a slender gold pen and made a note. Then she closed the notebook firmly and smiled.

"So," she said. "Where were we?"

"Great-Aunt Maisie?" Felix said cautiously. "Are you okay?"

"Okay?" Great-Aunt Maisie laughed. "Why, I'm marvelous, child!"

"But what happened?" he asked, confused.

Great-Aunt Maisie studied Felix's face carefully. She opened her mouth as if she might say something, but then she closed it again.

"You look wonderful," Maisie said. "And so . . . lively."

Great-Aunt Maisie nodded thoughtfully.

"Tell me," she said, "have you children had any more . . . adventures?"

Maisie shook her head. "We tried this morning. But it didn't work."

Great-Aunt Maisie gasped. "It must work," she said.

"But we don't know what we did in the first place," Maisie said.

The nurse came back in noisily, wheeling a cart with the tea and shortbread. Even though the silver teapot was tarnished, Maisie could see the engraved *P* on it.

"I suppose you want me to serve you, too," the nurse said sarcastically.

"Well, I'm not going to serve myself," Great-Aunt Maisie said.

With sharp, jerky motions, the nurse poured three cups of tea. Then she slammed the heavy teapot back down on the cart and stormed off.

Great-Aunt Maisie watched her go, sighing. "She wouldn't last a day at Elm Medona," she said. "Why, she didn't even add the cream and sugar."

Felix jumped up and busied himself doing just that. He opened the little sugar packets and poured them into the cups of tea, then opened the small containers of half-and-half.

"Maisie," Great-Aunt Maisie said, "make a note in my little notebook here, would you? I need some china teacups and saucers, the silver creamer and sugar bowl, and those darling little silver sugar tongs."

As Maisie jotted these things down, Great-Aunt Maisie smiled at her.

When she finished, Great-Aunt Maisie turned her attention back to Felix. "Tell me what you did this morning. We have to determine your error."

"Well," Felix said, "we picked up a document . . . blueprints actually—"

"We? Both of you?"

"Yes."

"And?"

"And nothing. I'm thinking maybe it was the time of day? Or that we didn't say the same things as the first time?"

Great-Aunt Maisie shooed at the air as if Felix were a fly.

"Open the drawer there by the bed," she ordered him.

Felix did as she asked.

"See the Fabergé egg inside?" she said.

"Wow!" Felix said. "This is amazing!"

He held up a pink enamel egg on a stand made of gold decorated with green-gold leaves, rubies, and pearls.

"Bring it here," Great-Aunt Maisie said, motioning him toward her.

"It's beautiful," Maisie said when Felix handed it to their aunt.

"This is a Fabergé egg that my father gave me on my tenth birthday," Great-Aunt Maisie said. "Czar

Alexander III commissioned the first one in 1885 as an Easter present to his wife, the czarina. That one had a little surprise inside—a golden hen hidden in a golden yolk. The hen wore a tiny crown with a ruby on it." Her face grew wistful. "So whimsical," she said. "So . . . surprising."

"Does this one have a surprise in it?" Felix asked. The egg was maybe the most beautiful thing he had ever seen.

Great-Aunt Maisie smiled. "It does," she said. "I haven't opened this egg since I was a young girl." Again, her voice grew wistful. "I swore then that I would never open it again. But you need to see what lies inside, in order to . . . understand Elm Medona."

CHAPTER 3

Anagrams

Maisie gingerly reached out to touch the clusters of pink pearls that formed flower petals across the egg.

"Oh, Great-Aunt Maisie!" she said. "These are peonies, aren't they?"

"That's right. The Pickworth peony," Great-Aunt Maisie said proudly. She carefully turned the egg upside down to reveal a pearl knob on the bottom. A tiny alphabet circled the knob.

Maisie peered closer. "Is there a secret combination to open the egg?"

"Smart girl," Great-Aunt Maisie said. "Instead of numbers, my father used letters. *Metaphoric kiwis,*" she added softly.

"Metaphoric what?" Felix said.

"Kiwis. My father first ate a kiwi in New Zealand when he lived with the Maori in 1892," Great-Aunt Maisie explained. "How he loved those funny, furry fruits with their sweet, green flesh."

"But what's *metaphoric kiwis*?" Felix asked.

"Write it down in my notebook," she told Maisie.

Maisie did as Great-Aunt Maisie asked, double-checking how to spell *metaphoric*.

"Do the letters mean anything to you?" Great-Aunt Maisie asked them.

Maisie and Felix stared at the letters for a long time, finding nothing there but the two strange words.

Finally, frustrated, Great-Aunt Maisie said, "It's an anagram!"

"Two words that have the same meaning?" Maisie asked.

"No, no, two words that have the same meaning are called synonyms. Honestly! Do *kiwis* and *metaphoric* have the same meaning?" She didn't wait for an answer. "An anagram is when the letters of a word or a phrase are rearranged to make new words or phrases. My father loved anagrams. In particular, he loved anagrams that had hidden meanings."

"So if we rearrange these letters," Felix said, excited, "not only will we find a new word, but that word will also have a secret meaning?"

"That's right," Great-Aunt Maisie said.

"What's the secret meaning in *metaphoric kiwis*?" Maisie asked.

Great-Aunt Maisie sighed deeply. "My goodness, don't you children know how to have fun? Figure it out! When you find the new word or phrase, you'll have the combination to open the egg."

"This is great," Felix said, already trying different orders for the letters.

"My father loved anagrams," Great-Aunt Maisie said again. "He used them all the time."

"Artichoke something?" Felix guessed, scribbling. "Artichoke swim . . . pi?"

Great-Aunt Maisie clapped her hands together. "Not even close!" she said gleefully.

Felix kept writing.

"Just tell us already," Maisie said, grumpy.

"Peach?" Felix asked hopefully.

"No!" Great-Aunt Maisie laughed.

"Itch . . . witch . . . worth . . . ," he tried.

"Pickworth!" Maisie shouted.

Great-Aunt Maisie pointed her finger at Maisie. "Smart girl!" she said, beaming.

Felix looked up from the notebook. "It's Maisie Pickworth, isn't it?" he said. "*Metaphoric kiwis* is an anagram for your name."

Great-Aunt Maisie held the Fabergé egg in her lap. She closed her eyes long enough for Maisie and Felix to think she had fallen asleep. But just as they decided that they might tiptoe out of the room, she opened her eyes slowly and gave them a sad smile.

"Sometimes it seems like just yesterday that I was a ten-year-old girl chasing my brother, Thorne, down the stairs and hallways of Elm Medona. Ah, the tea parties we had on the Great Lawn, in the gazebo. The adventures we had together."

As she spoke, her eyes grew teary, and Maisie reached over and gently held her hand.

"My brother got the matching egg," Great-Aunt Maisie continued. "His was pale blue enamel and decorated with lapis peacocks that had the most elaborate tails made of rubies and sapphires and emeralds. Thorne liked to say that his was much fancier, but I didn't care. I loved mine."

She held the egg up to admire it. The light from the window danced across it, making the peonies stand out even more.

"Of course," Great-Aunt Maisie said, lowering the egg into her lap again, "the real tragedy is the third egg. You see, my father had three eggs made when we were born. This one. Thorne's peacock egg. And the pineapple egg, which belonged to my mother. She died hours after giving birth to us. And, after she died, he put them all away in The Treasure Chest. On our tenth birthday, he presented Thorne and me with our eggs. Two years later, when we learned about the existence of a third egg, we searched The Treasure Chest for it. But it had disappeared."

"Who went in there who could take it?" Maisie asked.

Great-Aunt Maisie's lips tightened into a thin line. "Oh," she said, "there are a few suspects. Gilda LaRoche, one of my father's girlfriends. Mister Mars, my father's personal valet. And, of course, Thorne."

"Your brother!" Felix said, surprised.

"Ha! Some brother he turned out to be," Great-Aunt Maisie said.

She held up one hand. "But I've gone on far too long about all of this, and I'm growing weary. My point is *this* egg and what is in its secret compartment."

Great-Aunt Maisie gave the egg to Maisie. "Now that you know the code, spell it out by turning the pearl knob on the bottom to each letter. Just the way you would open a safe."

Carefully, Maisie turned the knob, pausing until she heard the soft click after each letter, until she had spelled out *metaphoric kiwis*. At the final *S*, the click was a little louder than the others. Maisie held her breath. Very slowly, the front of the egg opened, revealing a crystal peony.

"Inside that peony is what you need in The Treasure Chest. Surely you have one just like it," Great-Aunt Maisie said.

Maisie reached into the egg. The peony's petals lay open at the top, and she placed two fingers into that opening.

"But there's nothing there," she said.

"What?" Great-Aunt Maisie said harshly. She pushed Maisie's hand out of the way and lifted the egg to her face, jabbing her own gnarled fingers inside it.

Slowly, Great-Aunt Maisie lowered the egg back

to her lap. Her face had gone pale, and her eyes—teary just moments ago—were now steely.

Great-Aunt Maisie raised her fist and then slammed it hard on the arm of her chair. Then she said just one word, with a deep anger: "Thorne."

Just then, their mother walked into the room.

"What are you two doing here?" She was wearing her work clothes: a vaguely rumpled moss-green pantsuit, low-heeled pumps, and a briefcase slung over one shoulder.

Felix stood at the bedside table, where he had just returned the peony egg to the drawer.

"Just visiting," he said.

Maisie kneeled by their great-aunt's side.

"But how in the world did you get here?" their mother asked, her face creasing with worry.

"The bus?" Felix said tentatively.

"It was even easier than the subway, Mom," Maisie added quickly. "And supersafe."

"Did it ever occur to you two to call me before you did this?" their mother said. But even as she said it, she started to smile. "That is so sweet of you guys."

But when she saw Great-Aunt Maisie's pale, worn face, her smile vanished.

"Oh, darling," she said. "Are you having a bad day?"

Great-Aunt Maisie snarled, "I am having a horrible day."

"Oh, no," their mother said. She looked at Maisie and then at Felix. "You haven't worn her out, have you? Or upset her?"

They both shook their heads.

"I brought you those scones you like so much," their mother said, handing a white bakery box to Great-Aunt Maisie.

Great-Aunt Maisie swatted it away. "I would like you all to leave me alone."

"But—"

"All of you!" she growled.

The three of them quickly said their good-byes and headed toward the door.

"Children," Great-Aunt Maisie said, ringing the little silver bell hard, "without a piece from that vase, our journey is over. You must have one. You must."

"Now what do you want?" the nurse with the purple Crocs said, pushing past everyone.

"I want to go to bed," Great-Aunt Maisie said. "Now."

$

On the ride back to Elm Medona, their mother praised Maisie and Felix for their ingenuity in going to see Great-Aunt Maisie on their own.

"But the poor darling," she said. "She seemed to make so much progress, and now it looks like she's going backward again."

"She was lively this morning," Maisie said. "She talked about her father and her brother, Thorne, and her childhood."

"Mom," Felix asked, "whatever happened to Thorne?"

Their mother shrugged. "They had a big falling out when they were still very young. I've heard he lives in London, but I'm not sure."

Felix settled back in his seat. Great-Aunt Maisie had a way of getting him excited about things. Here he was, ready to time travel again, his mind full of mysteries. Why would Thorne steal what was in Great-Aunt Maisie's egg? Even worse, would he really steal the third egg? The Pickworths had more secrets than he'd ever imagined. Felix smiled to himself. And he had thought moving here would be dull!

"Has anyone ever tried to find him?" Maisie asked.

"Oh, I don't know," their mother said. "Once I asked Aunt Maisie if she wanted me to try to find him. This was when the Internet first started up, and I thought it might be fun to search for Thorne. But she practically took my head off, screaming about him being untrustworthy and possibly even a thief."

"The pineapple egg," Felix said. "That's what she was telling us about, too."

"Poor thing," their mother said. "At her age, she should be able to forgive and forget. It's likely that Thorne has passed away by now."

When they pulled into the driveway of Elm Medona, Maisie didn't get out of the car right away. Instead, she peered up at the mansion, to the place where The Treasure Chest was hidden.

Their mother took a bag of groceries from the trunk and headed up to the apartment.

Felix rapped on Maisie's window. "You coming?" he asked.

Maisie didn't answer him. She just kept looking up. Then she broke into a grin.

She opened the door, practically knocking into her brother.

"I got it!" she said.

"Got what?"

"What Great-Aunt Maisie was telling us. Remember? She said she had a piece, and we had to have one, too, or else we would never have been able to time travel. Well, we have that piece."

"We do?" Felix said, confused.

"My shard! From the Ming vase!"

"You think that really matters?" Felix said.

Maisie nodded. "Absolutely. There were two pieces missing from that vase. I have one, and I bet Great-Aunt Maisie had the other one. That's what she kept in that secret compartment. Thorne probably took it so he could continue to time travel."

"That's great, Maisie," Felix said. "But where is your shard?"

Maisie's face fell. "That's the only problem," she admitted. "I had it in the pocket of my fleece vest. But it wasn't there when I got dressed this morning."

"You're sure?" Felix asked.

"Yeah. I was going to take it out and put it in my jewelry box, but it was gone."

Now it was Felix's turn to get excited. "Mom did the laundry!" he said, already moving up the driveway to the door. "It must have fallen out in the washing machine!"

"Yes!" Maisie said, remembering.

She ran fast enough to reach the door before him. By the time he got halfway up the stairs, she had already gone into the apartment and was opening the laundry room door.

"Not here!" Maisie said when Felix ran in the laundry room, panting.

"Did you check the dryer?" he said. Without waiting for an answer, he opened the dryer door and looked inside, running his hands around it as he did.

"Nothing," he said.

"First you go visit Great-Aunt Maisie on your own. Now you want to do the laundry? You are definitely up to something," their mother said, stopping at the door.

"No, no," Maisie said so quickly that their mother narrowed her eyes even more suspiciously.

"I just lost something."

"In here?" their mother said.

"It was in my fleece pocket. I think it fell out in the wash," Maisie told her.

Their mother shrugged and moved the strap of her briefcase to her other shoulder.

"I emptied pockets into there," she said, pointing to a jelly jar on the shelf beside the detergent.

Maisie resisted the urge to frantically look inside the jar. She didn't want to raise their mother's curiosity even more.

"Great," she said, trying not to sound too enthusiastic.

Felix nodded.

"Okay," their mother said, studying their faces. "Well, I need to get back to the office for a couple of hours and finish this deposition. How about we get pizza when I get home?"

"Great," Maisie said again.

Their mother kissed them each good-bye on the top of their heads. Maisie and Felix stepped out of the laundry room to watch her walk through the kitchen and out the door. They waited until the door closed and they could no longer hear her heels against the floor.

Maisie grabbed the jelly jar from the shelf.

"Here it is!" she said triumphantly, holding the shard up for Felix to see. "Let's go!"

"Wait!" Felix said.

He went to the kitchen and checked the big bulletin board on the wall there. Beside the school lunch menu and a pizza delivery flyer under a yellow pushpin, he found the big preservation society calendar with the schedule for tours of Elm Medona marked in red. None were scheduled for that afternoon.

"Phew!" he said.

$

Felix and Maisie went back down the dumbwaiter, into the basement Kitchen, up the stairs that led to the Dining Room, and then out into the Grand Ballroom and up the Grand Staircase.

"Thank you," Felix whispered as they ran past the photograph of Great-Aunt Maisie.

Then he paused.

"Maisie?" he said. "Maybe Great-Aunt Maisie's shard is somewhere in the house. Maybe it's in her old room. Or even in Thorne's."

"What if it is?" Maisie said. "All we need is ours."

Felix hesitated. "I know," he said. "But she seemed so happy when she thought it was in that egg. Since we're already in here, couldn't we just poke around a little?"

"Well," Maisie said, considering.

"Five minutes?" Felix offered.

"I guess it would make her happy if we did find it," Maisie said, remembering how Clara Barton had told them to be kinder to Great-Aunt Maisie. Maisie sighed. "Five minutes."

Maisie and Felix walked down the long hallway that led to what used to be the family's bedrooms. First they passed Ariane Pickworth's room. The walls were a robin's-egg blue, and the ceiling was painted with white fluffy clouds. From each corner of the ceiling, a fat cherub smiled down at them.

"So creepy that she died in there," Felix said in a hushed voice.

He walked past the room quickly.

Beside Ariane's room was the nursery, a smaller room that still held two matching white cribs, two matching white rocking chairs, and two matching white chests of drawers. In fact, everything in that room was white.

Next came Thorne's bedroom.

"Should we poke around in there?" Felix asked. "I mean, if he took it, maybe he left it here."

Maisie sighed. *Two* rooms? They would never

get to The Treasure Chest. But then she pictured Great-Aunt Maisie and her delight at that egg and at sharing the anagram with them.

"Sure," she said.

Great-Uncle Thorne's room had a jungle mural painted on the walls, the dark green leaves reaching upward onto the ceiling. A rug made out of a lion's skin, with the head still attached and the mouth opened in a silent roar, took up most of the floor. The blanket on the bed was made of dark brown animal fur.

"Ugh," Maisie said, wrinkling her nose. "Who would ever sleep with all this dead animal stuff around them?"

Felix had already started to open drawers.

"Empty," he said.

Maisie opened the closet and peeked under the bed.

"No one's been in these rooms in years," she said. "Of course they've been emptied out."

"We'll still check Great-Aunt Maisie's real fast?"

"Fine," Maisie said impatiently.

She opened the door in the room that led to a bathroom with a claw-foot tub and a toilet with a big chain that had to be pulled for flushing. The towel racks had thick white towels on them, with the letters *TPP* monogrammed on some in dark red and *MAP* on the others in robin's-egg blue. Another door on the other side of the bathroom opened into Great-Aunt Maisie's room.

When Maisie and Felix walked in, they grew very quiet. It almost felt like being in church. Each item on the dresser—a heavy silver brush and comb and mirror—had the letters *MAP* engraved on them. One table held a dozen music boxes of different sizes and designs. Another had rows of dolls with real hair and creepy, realistic-looking faces staring back at them. The bed was so high that there was a little step stool to climb onto it. Under an elaborately embroidered canopy, the bed itself was stacked high with pillows.

"It looks like a little girl's room," Maisie said softly.

Felix nodded.

"I don't know why I feel so sad all of a sudden," Maisie said.

The walls here were a midnight blue, and the ceiling had constellations painted on it. Felix could identify the Big Dipper and Orion the Hunter.

"Look," Maisie said. Her fingers traced white lines that ran along one wall. Above the lines were numbers.

Felix studied them carefully. "They're longitudes and latitudes," he said finally.

"Four of them," Maisie said.

"I wonder where they lead to?" Felix said, imagining the globe that sat in his classroom with lines of longitude and latitude circling it.

Maisie pointed to another set of numbers.

"Dates," Felix said. Two of the dates were the same, and two were different and years older.

"Birthdays?" Maisie said.

"Great-Aunt Maisie's and Great-Uncle Thorne's?" Felix pointed to the two that were the same.

"We should go," Maisie said, feeling suddenly as if she were trespassing.

"But the shard could be in one of those music boxes or . . . or anywhere."

Maisie shook her head. "It's not," she said.

Somehow, Felix knew she was right.

$

For the second time that day, Maisie pressed the spot on the wall that opened it to reveal the staircase. As Felix followed his sister up the secret staircase, he remembered his mantra.

"Home," he whispered. "Home, home, home."

In The Treasure Chest, Maisie scanned the desk for the blueprints to the Holland Tunnel.

"I'm sure I put them right here," she said, lifting up the other items. She moved a porcupine quill, a compass, and a bouquet of dried flowers.

"We don't want those, anyway," Felix said, even as he repeated *home, home, home* in his mind.

"Yes, we do!" Maisie said, pushing things aside roughly. "They'll get us back to New York, just blocks from home."

With a sweep of her hand, a silver coin fell off the desk, landing with a loud thunk on the floor. The light bounced off it so that it practically glowed.

Felix bent to pick up the coin at the exact same time as Maisie did.

"Leave it alone," Maisie said, cross.

But he didn't.

They both touched the silver coin, and the room filled with the smells of salt water, coconut, and something sweet. A wind rushed past Maisie and Felix, carrying the sounds of sails flapping and palm tree leaves fluttering.

In an instant, they were gone.

CHAPTER 4

The Orphan Boy

Felix landed with a splash, grasping his glasses tight to his face. He opened his eyes and saw that he was underwater. Not just any water, either. This water was so clear that he could see Maisie's legs thrashing, a school of bright-yellow fish swimming past, and the soft, sandy bottom way, way beneath him. He swam upward, kicking his legs hard until he reached the surface. When his head finally popped out of the water, he took a big deep breath and looked around. In the distance lay a white-sand beach fringed with palm trees. But all around him, Felix saw nothing but beautiful turquoise water until Maisie appeared, sputtering and shaking the water from her hair, the coin pressed firmly in her fist.

"Over here!" Felix called, waving to her. He had certainly not expected this. Not at all. They were in the *ocean*!

Maisie looked about as angry as she could look. Felix watched her dive into the water and swim purposefully toward him. She was a good swimmer. And so was he. They had learned to swim when they were five at the Carmine Street Pool and had tied for first place in a relay race there when they were seven.

The sun shone bright and warm above them. Felix lay on his back and floated gently, gazing up at the clear, blue sky.

When Maisie reached him, she treaded water beside him.

"This," she said, "is not New York."

Felix smiled. "Nope," he said.

"This is all your fault," she said. "If you'd just let me find those blueprints, we wouldn't be in the middle of the ocean right now."

"First of all, we're not in the middle of the ocean. The beach is right over there. And second of all, this is actually kind of nice."

Maisie sighed. Clearly her brother was not going

to be any help in figuring out where they'd landed. Or why. She took a breath, stretched out her arms, and began to swim.

"Hey! Where are you going?" Felix called after her.

"To shore!" Maisie yelled back. And then she kept on swimming.

As she neared the beach, the waves grew large enough to carry her forward. She caught one just right and it lifted her and brought her right to shore, depositing her in a sandy heap. Riding that wave felt familiar. When the family used to go to Cape May, Maisie and her father would bodysurf for hours. She liked tumbling in the water, then landing on the beach beside her father, laughing and spitting salt water. She liked how tired she'd get by the end of the afternoon, how they would collapse on the beach blanket and close their eyes, how the smells of suntan lotion and fried foods and salt surrounded her. Even lying still, Maisie would still feel like she was moving through the cold Atlantic Ocean.

Maisie stood. *This* water wasn't cold at all. In fact, it was as warm as bathwater. She looked at the sugar-white sand and the tall palm trees.

Maybe they hadn't landed in the Atlantic Ocean, she realized. Maisie tried to picture a map of the United States. A whole bunch of states had palm trees and warm water. Like . . . Florida . . . and . . . definitely some other ones. *Maybe this is the Atlantic Ocean, but way down south*, she thought, walking up to the beach, her feet sinking in the soft sand as she did.

The beach seemed to stretch forever, and Maisie couldn't see anyone else on it. A palm tree lay on its side as if it had been knocked over, but otherwise the beach was empty. Maisie sat on the trunk of the fallen tree and pondered their situation. An empty beach, somewhere tropical. Another thought hit her. Not only didn't she know *where* they'd landed, she also had no idea *when* they'd landed. For all she knew, this place was completely deserted. Or inhabited by angry natives. Nervous, she looked around for clues. But there was nothing but this long, white-sand beach and the turquoise water and Felix goofing around in it, diving and splashing like they were in Cape May on vacation with their parents instead of stranded here.

Think, Maisie told herself. Last time, they'd

landed in that barn and Clara Barton had appeared immediately. Logically, someone would appear here, too, she decided. Any minute. Someone who needed the coin. That made her feel better. Maisie smiled, pleased with herself. They didn't have to do anything except wait right here. Any minute now, a person would walk up to them and things would start to make sense. She lifted her face toward the sun. Her mother would kill her for not using sunscreen, but Maisie had no choice. All she could do was hope her nose didn't get too red and her freckles didn't multiply too much.

Time passed this way. Maisie sat on the trunk of the palm tree, waiting. Felix played around in the water. The sun rose higher and the day grew hotter, until eventually Maisie began to worry and Felix got bored and came out of the ocean and up the beach to where his sister had started to pace.

"We've been here a long time," she said.

"And I'm starving," Felix said.

Maisie's stomach grumbled. "I thought for sure someone would show up."

Felix stared off down the length of the beach. "It's pretty deserted," he said finally.

"Do you think we're on a desert island?" Maisie asked.

Felix chewed on his bottom lip, which had started to get chapped from the salt and sun. "I don't know," he concluded. Then he said, "I need lunch and ChapStick."

"They don't have ChapStick on desert islands," Maisie said miserably.

"They don't have food, either. Just coconuts and fish you have to catch with your bare hands," Felix said, starting to get nervous.

"Well," Maisie said, "there's only one thing we can do: explore."

"What if it's dangerous out there? What if there's wild animals or headhunters or—"

"We can't just stay here like this forever. We'll starve."

"Maisie?" Felix said softly. "Where do you think *here* is?"

She swallowed hard. "Maybe Florida?"

Felix nodded. "Florida wouldn't be so bad."

Maisie hoped he didn't ask the next logical question.

But he did.

"*When* do you think it is?" he asked.

Their eyes met. Felix waited.

Then Maisie said, "I have absolutely no idea."

Maisie and Felix began to walk. After some discussion on which direction would be best, they decided it didn't matter. Neither left nor right held any more promise than the other. They just started walking in the direction of the sun, which had reached straight overhead and now was to their right.

They walked for a very long time and still came upon nothing but more white sand, more palm trees, and more fallen trees. Neither of them spoke. What was there to say? They were hungry and both of them were more than a little afraid, even though the beach was beautiful and the weather warm and lovely, with just the right amount of breeze to keep them from getting too hot.

Eventually the beach curved and they saw in the near distance a harbor filled with boats.

"We're saved!" Felix said happily. Boats meant people and restaurants.

But seeing boats didn't make Maisie feel optimistic. Especially *those* boats. Oh, there were a lot of them, but each and every one was a sailboat. Large, with tall masts and weathered tan sails, these boats looked old. Really old. Like maybe a hundred years old. Or more.

"These look like the tall ships," she said.

The tall ships had passed through New York Harbor a few years ago. Their parents had taken them down to Battery Park to watch them sail past. They'd had to listen to some boring guy give the history of tall ships. Some of them were modern and still used today. But the term originally referred to ships from long ago. Wooden sailing ships. Like the ones Maisie was looking at right then.

Relieved, Felix grinned. "We're at a tall ship festival?"

"I don't think it's a festival," Maisie said.

They had reached the end of the sandy beach and had come to a wooden dock with a steep staircase leading up to the boats and the street.

"Careful," Maisie said as they climbed the stairs. She pointed to where the wood had rotted and left gaping holes, the water shining through them.

The air stunk of fish and garbage and things rotting in the sun, and the noise level increased as they made their way up. Men shouted. Metal clanged. Sails flapped. Water smacked the dock.

It began to sink in with Felix that these tall ships were actual, working boats. Which meant they had gone back to a time when sailing ships carried cargo and traveled from harbor to harbor. But exactly when was that?

At the top of the stairs, Maisie and Felix stopped to take in the scene.

Men with bulging muscles pulled thick ropes and carried enormous crates both off of and onto ships. Other men gathered, bickering and shouting, pointing at this ship or that crate.

"At least they're speaking English," Maisie whispered.

English, yes. Felix heard British accents and other accents—maybe German? Dutch?—that he didn't understand, but no one sounded American.

The street that bordered the harbor had many small, low buildings and the appearance of a town of sorts.

"Let's cross the street," Maisie said.

As they made their way through the crowd, they saw black women squatting by the side of the road selling food from baskets. Pineapples cut into chunks, mangos, strips of coconut, fried fritters, and dried fish. Maisie and Felix paused, their mouths watering.

One of the women, dressed in a bright-yellow cotton dress with big, red flowers on it and a bandana wrapped around her head, motioned to them.

"My conch the freshest here, children," she said.

Her basket held crisp fritters, glistening with oil.

"We don't have any money," Maisie said, her stomach aching with hunger pangs.

"Too bad," the woman said. She turned her attention to other people passing by.

"Conch fritters here," she called to them.

Maisie and Felix lingered, the smell of her fritters mixing with that of ripe pineapple.

"Wait a minute," Felix said. "We do have money."

Maisie looked at him, confused. Then she broke into a grin.

"Ma'am," she said to the woman. "Here." She held out the heavy silver coin.

The woman took it and brought it close to her eyes. Then anger flashed across her face.

"What kind of fool you think I am?" she said.

"This is a counterfeit dollar." She tapped the coin with her finger. "1794?"

Maisie and Felix looked at each other.

The woman plopped the coin back in Maisie's hand. "Off with you," she said, shaking her head. "1794. How am I going to use money from a year that hasn't even happened yet?"

"It's *earlier* than 1794?" Felix whispered to his sister.

"And she's not who we're looking for," Maisie whispered back.

The woman, realizing they hadn't gone, studied their faces openly.

"You hungry children, yes?" she said gently.

They nodded.

The woman studied them. "All dressed in funny-looking clothes. And those funny-looking clothes all wet."

Maisie returned the woman's gaze.

"So many hungry children since the hurricane," she said, shaking her head sadly.

A hurricane! That explained why so many trees had been knocked down. Felix sighed, relieved they hadn't turned up a week earlier.

"Take my conch fritters, hungry children," the woman said.

Maisie and Felix each took a warm fritter.

"Thank you," Felix said.

The woman nodded, satisfied.

Maisie waited. Would something else happen?

But the woman seemed to have already forgotten them. She turned to three men who counted money and placed it in her hand, taking several fritters from her basket.

Disappointed, Maisie walked away.

The fritters tasted salty and delicious. It took three bites to finish them off. Felix licked his fingers while they continued on their way. People of all sizes and shapes and colors pressed together. Now the smell of sweat and animals mixed with all the other terrible smells. Felix covered his nose and mouth with his hand, breathing in the ocean smell on it. The fritter, which had tasted so good, turned sour in his stomach. Finally, they broke through the crowd and stood at the edge of the road, the harbor behind them and the row of buildings across the street.

"I thought someone would come up to us back there," Maisie admitted. "When we landed in that barn, Clara showed up right away. But it seems like we're really on our own this time."

Felix didn't want to believe that. "Someone will show up. You'll see," he said, trying to convince himself as well as his sister.

"Let's just go into one of these stores and see if we can figure out where we are," Maisie said.

"Good idea."

He let her lead the way because he knew that would make her feel better. As they crossed the street, Felix noted that instead of cars, carriages lined one side of the dirt street, and here and there sat piles of horse poop, which added to the smell. There didn't seem to be any people, either, unlike the harbor that had been so crowded.

Maisie paused, trying to figure out which building to go into. They all looked pretty much the same, so she finally chose the one closest to them, which was also the largest. The numbers on it were 56-57, and the sign outside said BEEKMAN AND CRUGER. She pushed open the wooden door and stepped inside, Felix close behind her. It was dark and cool, and it took a minute for her eyes to adjust.

Bolts of fabric filled shelves on one wall; heavy

brown jugs stood in front of them; boxes held tools, rope, yarn, and pieces of wood.

"A general store," Felix said, running his hands along burlap bags of rice and dried beans.

"Hello?" Maisie called.

Even though the door had been unlocked, the store appeared to be empty. Outside, behind it, Maisie could see a large enclosed yard. But it, too, was empty.

"Maybe someone's upstairs," Felix said, pointing to a stairway near where they'd entered.

They went upstairs and opened another door at the top. In a large office, a teenage boy sat on a stool at a high desk, writing with a gray feather pen in an enormous open book.

He didn't notice them.

Maisie and Felix waited. The boy had reddish hair, high cheekbones, and what their mother would call a strong chin. He looked very serious bent over the book like that.

Maisie cleared her throat.

Slowly, the boy looked up from the book to Maisie and Felix. His violet-blue eyes swept over them, sizing them up.

"Yes?" he said finally.

"I wonder," Maisie began.

The boy climbed off his stool and walked boldly toward them. He wasn't very tall, only a few inches taller than Maisie. But he had such confidence that he seemed to be much taller.

"Yes?" he said again, standing in front of them now.

Maisie swallowed hard. The boy made her feel all discombobulated.

Felix glanced at his sister, startled. She was blushing! He had never seen any boy make her blush before.

"Could you please tell us the date?" Felix said, taking over.

The boy laughed. "You've come in here to find out the date?"

"Yes," Felix said.

"It's October the second. 1772."

"1772?" Felix said, his mind racing. The Declaration of Independence was signed on July 4, 1776. *Four years from now*, he thought.

"Yes," the boy said, curious now. "Have you been away at sea?"

"Yes!" Maisie said, delighted. "We have! How did you know?"

He pointed at Maisie's blue jeans. "You're dressed like sailors," he said. The boy folded his arms. "You've been away at sea and landed here on Saint Croix because . . . ?"

"Saint Croix!" Maisie said, even more delighted. She didn't know anything at all about Saint Croix except that it was somewhere in the Caribbean.

"Have you landed in the wrong place?" the boy said.

"Yes." Maisie laughed. "You could say that."

"We have ships that go all over the world," the boy bragged. "Perhaps I can help you get where you need to be."

"Really?" Maisie said. "You can rescue us?"

The boy puffed up his chest. "I can do anything," he boasted.

"Who are you that you can do anything at all?" Maisie said.

"Alexander Hamilton," the boy said proudly, as if it meant something.

CHAPTER 5

Alexander Hamilton

This guy is so full of himself, Maisie thought. Even as she thought it, her stomach did a funny little tumble. Ever since first grade, when Felix announced he was in love with Tamara Berkowitz and intended to marry her, Felix could not help getting crushes on girls. Sarah Thacher from the Bleecker Playground. Adrienne Stone from the Carmine Street Pool. Charlotte Weinberg from Little League. And, Maisie suspected, that girl Lily from his class now.

But Maisie found boys mostly annoying, sometimes smelly, and, very rarely, fun to hang out with. So why in the world did this Alexander Hamilton, who strutted like a rooster, make her stomach do this tumble and her hands get kind of clammy? Was this what Felix felt for all those girls?

"I'm Felix Robbins," Felix was saying, "and this is my sister, Maisie."

"Where did you two come from?" Alexander asked.

Felix waited for Maisie to answer. She always had something to say. But she just stood there, looking a little pale and a lot confused.

"Um . . . Rhode Island?" Felix said.

Delight filled Alexander's face. "The colonies?" he said.

"I . . . I guess so," Felix said thoughtfully, realizing that, of course, if the Declaration of Independence hadn't been signed yet, the United States didn't exist. "Yes. The colonies."

"You must tell me everything about them," Alexander said, slapping Felix on the back. "Of course, New York is the one that truly interests me. My friend Neddy is there at King's College."

"There's no such college," Maisie blurted, finally able to find her voice.

Alexander laughed. "Don't tell Neddy that. He's been studying there for two years."

"We're *from* New York," Maisie said. "King's College—"

Alexander pointed a finger at her. "I thought you were from Rhode Island," he said.

"We are now," Maisie said. "We moved there from New York."

"Then you know it's between Barclay and Murray Street. Neddy says it sits on a bluff overlooking the Hudson." Alexander sighed. "What I would give to get there myself."

"Me too!" Maisie said, drawn even more to this young man.

"Ah!" he said, nodding. "So you are trying to get back there?"

"More than anything," Maisie said. "Our mother wants to be in Rhode Island," she muttered.

Sadness crossed Alexander's face. But then he took a breath and forced a smile at them.

"I'll buy you some of Saint Croix's best fish if you'll tell me all about New York. And Rhode Island, too," he said.

"That would be great," Felix said, his stomach grumbling. "We haven't eaten in a while."

Alexander threw his arm around Felix's shoulder.

"Come then," he said. "Right across King's Street on the wharf we can get the freshest fish in Christiansted."

They stepped back outside into the sunlight.

"Christiansted is the capital?" Felix asked. He kind of wished Alexander would take his arm off his shoulder, but the boy kept Felix firmly in his grasp.

"The capital of all nineteen miles of this island," Alexander said. He motioned to the hills that rose above the town. "There are three hundred and eighty-one plantations up there, covering about thirty thousand acres."

"What do they grow?" Felix asked.

"Sugar, mostly. But cotton, too. And coffee," Alexander said.

The street was now even more crowded, but Alexander seemed to know everyone. Passing men tipped their hats to him or wished him a good day.

"You're pretty popular," Maisie said as they pushed through the crowd.

"Yes," Alexander said proudly. "I know just about everyone on the island. And I know about everything, too. I ran the entire business for Mr. Cruger when he got sick last year," Alexander continued boasting.

"For six months! I had to negotiate prices for cargo shipments to and from New York, collect the monies. Everything involved with imports and exports. When he came back from New York in March, he told me that without me he couldn't have kept things going." Alexander straightened his back. "And all this at only seventeen years old. Impressive, eh?"

"It looked like you were just a bookkeeper or something," Maisie said.

Alexander's violet eyes flared angrily. "I'm back to my old job as a clerk," he said. "But not for long. Just watch me."

By this time they had reached the wharf again, and the smell of fish and sweat was even stronger in the afternoon sun and heat.

"Which ship did you arrive on?" Alexander asked them.

Maisie and Felix exchanged a glance.

"It's gone already," Maisie said.

Alexander looked out at the ships crowding the harbor.

"How odd to arrive and depart so quickly," he said. "It was a bark?"

When they didn't answer, he said, "A schooner?"

Felix laughed nervously. "I'm not sure."

Alexander pointed to a large ship that looked very much like one of the tall ships that had sailed through New York Harbor.

"That ship there is a schooner. The square rigged one beside it is a bark. Barks have three or more masts."

Felix tried to look interested, but all he wanted was that fish they'd been promised. When Alexander kept talking, Felix groaned. This guy might never shut up.

"They say that when the first one was launched in the colony of Massachusetts half a century ago, someone watching said, 'Oh, how she scoons!'" Alexander said. "In Scottish, *scoons* means to skip or skim over water. Well, the builder of that ship, Captain Andrew Robinson, replied, 'A schooner let her be then!'"

Maisie thought she could listen to this Alexander Hamilton talk forever. He was a show-off and full of himself, but he was charming just the same.

"What's that one?" she asked him, just to keep him talking. Maisie pointed to a smaller ship.

Felix glared at his sister.

"The small one?" Alexander asked. "That's a sloop."

"Wow!" Felix said. "Great! Is that fish you were telling us about around here somewhere?"

"This way," Alexander said, leading them past the people hawking food and wares.

He stopped at the small stand of a woman who was dropping fish dusted with flour into bubbling oil.

"Alexander," she said, smiling at him. "How is Mr. Cruger treating you?"

"Just fine, Miss Liza," he said. "My new friends here need to try the best fish in Christiansted."

Miss Liza blushed. "Go on with you," she said.

She lifted several pieces of fish from the oil with a small wire basket and placed them in cones made from newspaper.

"One for yourself, too, I imagine?"

Alexander laughed his hearty laugh. "You know I cannot resist your fish," he said.

Miss Liza made a third cone and added fish to it.

As he took a few coins from his pocket, Maisie got a good look at them. No wonder the conch lady had looked so suspicious. These coins were smaller and lighter, nothing like the silver dollar she now had nestled in the front pocket of her jeans.

Alexander handed a cone of fish to Maisie and then one to Felix. The third cone he lifted up, pretending to read the newspaper.

"This one doesn't have my poem in it, I trust," he joked. "I hope it's not meant to hold fish. Even fish as good as yours."

Miss Liza grinned at him. "That poem, Alexander, made me blush. And I understand you lied about your age to the *Gazette*."

"Only by a year," Alexander said.

Miss Liza shook her head. "Alexander!" she pretended to scold.

After good-byes and thank-yous, Alexander brought Maisie and Felix to a dock where they could sit away from the crowds, facing the ocean.

"She puts sugar in the batter," Alexander said as he took a bite of fish. "That's what makes it so delicious."

It *was* delicious. Crunchy and sweet, the white fish inside flaky and fresh.

"Would you like to hear my poem?" Alexander asked them. "The one that ran in the *Gazette*?"

"I have a feeling you're going to recite it no matter what we say," Felix said.

Alexander cleared his throat, then began in a

deep, strong voice, "In yonder mead my love I found . . ."

As he recited the poem, Felix pretended to listen. But the poem wasn't to his liking. It was overly romantic, something about a shepherd boy falling in love.

When Alexander finished, Maisie applauded enthusiastically. "I love your rhymes," she said.

Felix snorted. Maisie didn't care about rhymes or poetry. Why was she acting like this?

"Yes," Alexander said, "they are good in that one. My second published poem was a bit more ribald."

"Ribald?" Maisie said, disappointed she didn't know the word.

"Randy," Felix said.

"My essay, 'Rules for the Statesman,' which was published more recently, is a bit more serious," Alexander said, talking to Maisie as if Felix weren't even there. "In it, I advocate for the British system of a prime minister with cabinet members as the best way to govern. What do you think about that system?"

"Yes, Maisie," Felix said, stifling a laugh, "what do you think about that system?" He wondered what in the world Alexander even meant.

"Well, it sure looks like it works, doesn't it?" she said, hoping she sounded like she knew what she was talking about.

Alexander's face brightened. "Exactly!" he said.

Felix rolled his eyes.

"I suppose you know about the hurricane that hit here in August?" Alexander asked Maisie.

She nodded solemnly, causing Felix to roll his eyes again.

"It was the worst hurricane to ever hit our little island," Alexander said softly. "The winds blew relentlessly for at least six hours. Ships were blown out of the water and were lying right there and there," he said, indicating with his head. "The tides rose fourteen feet higher than usual, and crops from the hills were uprooted and blown into the streets here."

"How terrible," Maisie said.

"I've written an account of it," Alexander boasted. "I sent it to my father on Saint Kitts, but Reverend Knox also read it, and he thinks the *Gazette* might run it."

"So you're a real writer?" Maisie said.

Felix shuddered at the way his sister was fawning over this show-off.

"Yes," Alexander said, grinning. "But I think I'll become a physician some day, like Neddy. If I can ever get to New York."

Maisie sighed. "I understand the frustration there," she said.

Alexander stood and brushed off his trousers.

"I need to get back to work now," he said. "We've talked about poetry and ships, but I still know nothing more about New York." He pointed his finger at Maisie. "When we meet again, you will give me details, won't you?"

Maisie blushed. She was grateful the opportunity hadn't come up to talk about New York. How could she explain subways and Times Square and how pretty the Empire State Building looked all lit up at night? No matter how hard she tried, she could not think of anything to tell Alexander here in 1772 that would make any sense to him.

"I will," Maisie said. "Lots of details."

Alexander smiled. "It's been very nice to meet you both."

He bowed, taking Maisie's hand and kissing it.

Maisie gasped, and when he released her hand, she stared at it as if it didn't belong to her.

Alexander shook Felix's hand. Then, without another word, he turned and walked away.

Maisie and Felix watched him go, until he got swallowed up in the crowd.

Felix turned to his sister.

"Well, Maisie," he said. "If he's the guy we're supposed to give that silver dollar to, he just disappeared."

CHAPTER 6

Slave Auction

Maisie and Felix looked at each other.

"Now what are we supposed to do?" Felix said.

"I have no idea," Maisie said. She could not believe what had just happened to them. Alexander Hamilton had walked away, leaving them alone on the island of Saint Croix in 1772.

"Maybe he's not the one we're here to meet," Felix offered.

Maisie considered this possibility. If it wasn't him, then who was it? And how were they supposed to find that person?

"Let's look at the coin," Felix said. "Maybe there's a clue on it."

Maisie dug into the pocket of her jeans, where

she'd tucked the shard and the coin for safety as soon as she'd landed in the water.

"It's just a silver dollar," she said, holding it out in her palm.

Felix took it from her, surprised by how heavy it felt. It was actually beautiful. One side had a picture of a woman with flowing hair and the word LIBERTY on it. The other side had a graceful bald eagle surrounded by a wreath of leaves. The words HUNDRED CENTS ONE DOLLAR OR UNIT were printed on the edge of it.

"1794," Felix said, studying it.

"So?" Maisie said, frustrated. "Big deal."

Felix sighed. "Do you think Alexander Hamilton had anything to do with money?"

"How am I supposed to know?" Maisie said. "Anyway, that coin is a US coin, and we're here in the Caribbean. That doesn't make any sense."

"But it's dated twenty-two years from now. Anything could happen in twenty-two years," Felix said.

"I feel like he's the person we're supposed to give it to," Maisie said. "If we wander too far from him, he might not be able to find us."

"Maybe we should just find a place to wait and

see what happens," Felix said, relieved. He wasn't eager to venture into the island without knowing anything about it.

He looked at the crowded wharf and across the street where the town's businesses stood, and then finally up the hills at the plantations. None of it seemed very appealing to him.

"The beach?" Maisie offered.

"Okay," Felix said. He wasn't thrilled at the idea of spending the night there, either. But what choice did they have?

They walked back along the wharf. Maisie liked looking out at the ships and knowing which one was a schooner and which was a bark. The schooners were the biggest and probably the ones that went across the ocean, to Holland and England and . . .

"Wait a minute!" Maisie said, grabbing her brother's arm. "Maybe one of those schooners is sailing to New York."

"Oh no," Felix said. "I'm not getting on a ship and sailing across the Atlantic Ocean."

"But we wanted to get back to New York, right? Somehow things got mixed up and we landed here, but that's our way back," she said, pointing at the biggest ship of all. "Right there."

Before Felix could protest more, Maisie ran down the dock and stopped a sailor there.

"Do any of these ships sail to New York?" she asked him.

The tall, blond man didn't even pause as he answered. "You just missed one. Next one's in two days."

Excited, Maisie ran back to Felix, who stood at the end of the dock waiting for her.

"I heard him," Felix said. The last thing he wanted was to get on one of these ships. They didn't have any navigation system except the stars. And weren't there pirates out there? And storms? Maybe even hurricanes?

"So we just need to find a place to spend the next couple of days, and then we are headed to New York. Who needs Alexander Hamilton, anyway?"

"That doesn't make sense, Maisie," Felix insisted. "I thought *we* needed him. If he's supposed to have the coin, we won't be able to get home unless we give it to him."

"Fine," she said. "When we see him, we'll give him the dumb coin, and then we'll get on that ship to New York."

"And then how do we get back to the present? To Mom?"

Maisie didn't answer him. Instead, she began to walk purposefully toward the beach. Felix followed her. He had one thought in his mind: How could he figure out a way back before his sister made him get on that ship?

$

Maisie had watched enough reality television to know they needed to build a shelter of some kind and try to find some food and water. Knowing that they would be headed for New York in a couple of days made the idea of sleeping on the beach almost fun.

"What an adventure, huh?" she said to Felix, who looked about as miserable as she'd ever seen him. "Stop sulking," she told him. "It's warm and dry, and we always wanted Mom and Dad to take us on a cruise or something, didn't we? So here we are, on a Caribbean island."

"We have no food, no bed, and no money," Felix said, counting off on his fingers as he spoke.

"We have the coin," Maisie reminded him.

"Right. Somebody's going to take a coin that

doesn't even go into circulation for over twenty years."

"Come on," Maisie said, elbowing him playfully. "This is probably the only Caribbean vacation we'll ever get."

"This is not a vacation!" Felix said.

But Maisie had run ahead of him, onto the sugar-white sand and straight into the turquoise water.

He had no choice but to dive in after her. For now, anyway, they were stuck here until he figured out a way home. He took off his glasses and held them tightly in his hand.

The water was even warmer than before. Felix dived down and opened his eyes. Schools of colorful fish swam around him. Here, bright yellow and white striped ones. Over there, electric-blue ones. In the distance, he could make out a coral reef stretching toward him.

Slowly, he made his way to the surface, watching the air bubbles rise with him. He came up right beside his sister, who was treading water and squinting into the distance.

"Look," she said.

Felix squinted, too, in the direction where Maisie was looking. There, on the horizon, he could just make out the silhouettes of dolphins leaping into the air. Beneath the water, Maisie's hand found his and held it, squeezing tight.

$

On television shows, the contestants found twigs and things to build shelters. They caught fish with their hands and made fire by rubbing two stones together. Maisie and Felix were not so clever. They could find only palm trees and coconuts and lots of seashells.

"I guess we'll just have to sleep out in the open," Maisie said, trying to still sound optimistic.

After swimming for a long time, they had dried off on the beach, then set off to find all the things they would need to get them through the next couple of days. But now the sky was turning red and violet, and they sat leaning against one of the fallen palm trees, preparing for a night without any food or shelter.

"Do you think there are wild animals out here?" Felix whispered.

Maisie had no idea. But she said, "No, not on the beach."

He picked up a coconut.

"If we could get this open, we'd have something to eat."

Actually, Felix hated coconut. He didn't like macaroons or Almond Joys or the coconut shrimp his father used to make. But he was hungry enough to eat almost anything. It seemed like a million years since he'd eaten that fried fish, and his stomach was grumbling loudly again now.

"Pound it against the tree trunk," Maisie suggested.

Felix lifted the coconut and slammed it down as hard as he could against the tree.

Nothing.

He tried again, but the hard shell didn't even crack a little.

"Let me try," Maisie said.

She didn't have any luck, either.

Felix put his hands over hers, and the two of them used all the force they could muster to crash that coconut down. This time it got away from them and skittered onto the sand.

"Hopeless." Felix groaned.

"You don't even like coconut," Maisie said, which made them both laugh.

Dusk had fallen, and a light buzzing filled the air.

"What the—" Maisie began, but the sharp sting of a mosquito on her neck cut her short.

"Mosquitoes!" Felix said, jumping up and swatting his legs.

A small, angry cloud of mosquitoes descended on them, stinging their arms and legs and necks.

Felix slapped at them, but it was no use. When he blinked, he felt mosquitoes on his eyelids.

"Aaaaaarrrrggghhh!" he screamed.

"Run!" Maisie said, batting her arms as if she could knock the mosquitoes out of the air.

The two of them took off, fast, down the beach and back toward the lights of Christiansted.

$

Standing in front of the locked door of Beekman and Cruger, Maisie and Felix tried to figure out how they could find Alexander Hamilton again. King's Street had emptied out now, the horses and carriages long gone. Candles flickered in some windows in the houses up the street adjacent to it, but even as they stood wondering what to do, the lights that had led them back here were slowly extinguished. Felix was thinking about the mosquito bites that ringed his ankles and climbed up his calves. Wasn't Saint Croix in the tropics? And didn't the mosquitoes in the tropics carry diseases like malaria or yellow fever or worse? Maybe even the plague?

Despite himself, he whined, "What if we get yellow fever?"

"Yellow fever!" Maisie said. "Let's concentrate on our real problems. Like having nowhere to sleep on this dark, creepy island."

Felix swallowed hard. Did he have a sore throat? Was that a sign of some deadly tropical disease?

"I think I have a sore throat," he said.

"No, you don't," Maisie said. She caught sight of a man leaving the building next door to Beekman and Cruger, locking the door, and walking slowly up King's Street.

"Excuse me," she said, stepping into his path, "do you know where the Hamiltons live?"

The man took a step back into the remaining lamplight, so as to better see Maisie.

"Are you sure you mean the Hamiltons?" he asked her.

Maisie nodded. "Alexander's family," she said, in

case Hamilton was the most common name on Saint Croix.

The man shook his head. "There is no Hamilton family," he said. He had a big, bushy mustache and a very round, red face. "The boy lives with the Stevenses. His friend Neddy's parents."

The man turned to continue on his way, but Maisie said, "Why does he live with them instead of his own family?"

Stopping, the man sighed and shook his head. "The father, that would be James Hamilton, left for Saint Kitts years ago and hasn't been seen around here since. Even when Rachel died, he didn't come back."

"Rachel?" Maisie asked him.

Felix rolled his eyes. Why did she need to know every single detail about Alexander Hamilton? All they really needed was to find the Stevenses' house.

But, of course, the man was droning on. "Alexander's mother. Rachel. She died in '68, poor thing. Both she and the boy, Alexander, got yellow fever."

Felix gasped. His hands went up to his throat. It *did* hurt, he decided.

"Yellow fever?" he managed to say. "It's here? On this island?"

"It comes every year," the man said, nodding. "She called Doctor Heering," he continued, "and he did his best. They say the chicken broth the nurse gave her seemed to help for a bit, but three days later she died. The boy survived. But they took everything from him and his brother, everything except her books. He's a smart one, that Alexander. And loves to read."

For a moment, the man grew quiet.

"Yellow fever comes every year?" Felix managed to croak.

The man nodded again.

"Can't you control the mosquitoes?"

At this, the man laughed. "Mosquitoes? What would they have to do with yellow fever?"

Of course, Felix realized, scratching at his mosquito-bitten knees. They hadn't figured out yet that mosquitoes carried yellow fever.

The man began to walk away again, then turned back to the children.

"The Stevenses' house," he said. "Up the street here."

Without being asked, Maisie and Felix followed him.

The sidewalks were made of inlaid tiles, and the houses—the colors of sherbet—had overhanging balconies with flowers hanging from them in long trellises. The air smelled sweet, and once again, Maisie started to relax.

"What are the symptoms of yellow fever?" Felix whispered to his sister.

But it was the man who answered. "Well," he said, "there's the fever itself. And the vomiting. But it doesn't come until winter. Seems to start right around Christmas every year."

Relieved, Felix said, "Why didn't you say so?"

The man didn't answer him. Instead, he pointed to a raspberry house. "The Stevenses' home," he said.

The house appeared to be dark, as if everyone in it had gone to sleep.

"That light burning back there," the man said, "that would be Alexander. Probably studying."

Maisie saw it now, the one light in the room farthest from the street.

The man tipped his hat at Maisie and Felix.

"Good night then," he said, and continued up the street.

"We can't wake them up," Felix said, hoping his sister would, in fact, do just that. The thought of a bed and some food and water made him almost brave enough to do it himself.

"No," Maisie agreed. "But there's a barn back there. We could sleep in there." She elbowed her brother playfully. "Like at the Bartons!"

"Who would have thought that time traveling always dropped you in a barn?" Felix laughed.

He thought a minute, then he said, "You could throw pebbles up at Alexander's window," Felix suggested. They did that in the movies sometimes, and he always had wanted to try it himself.

"I'm not going to do that," she said.

"Why not?"

"He might get mad at me," Maisie said.

"Who cares if he's mad at you!" Felix said. His sister never cared about things like that.

"I care!" she said. "And I'm sleeping in that barn. If you want to throw pebbles at his window, be my guest."

She walked purposefully toward the barn. Felix

could tell there was no changing her mind, so he walked right behind her.

The barn smelled awful, though not as bad as the wharf had. It was small, with a couple of horses in a stable and a goat in the main part. If they were going to sleep here, they would have to share the space with that goat.

"At least the hay is soft," Felix said, trying to be optimistic.

Maisie looked at the goat. The goat eyed her warily.

"Just great," she muttered.

Maisie and Felix curled up in opposite corners, and even though the hay was scratchy, the barn was smelly, and the goat was curious, they fell asleep immediately.

$

Felix woke up the next morning with a goat staring right in his face. He'd never been this close to a goat, except for at the petting zoo in Central Park. *The goat is actually kind of cute,* Felix thought. But when he went to pet it, the goat opened his mouth and attempted to chomp on Felix's hand.

"Maisie," Felix said, "wake up or we might be this goat's breakfast."

Maisie groaned. "Don't even say the word *breakfast* unless you have some."

"I wish," Felix said. "Maybe your boyfriend can get us something to eat."

In a flash, Maisie was standing over him, eyes on fire, nostrils flaring. "He's not my boyfriend," she said.

"Okay, okay," Felix said, getting to his feet.

As soon as he stood up, the goat butted him, knocking him back to the ground.

"Ouch!" Felix said, rubbing his back.

Maisie pulled him up and hurried him away before the goat repeated its attack. Outside, the sun was already hot, the air still.

"Go and knock on the door," Maisie said, nudging Felix toward the house. "Ask for Alexander."

"I'm not doing that!"

"I just saved you from a ferocious goat," Maisie said. "Now it's your turn."

Felix stared at the door, trying to summon his courage.

Before he even came close to approaching it, the door flew open and a woman stepped out. She was wearing a long dress and apron, and she carried a rug in one hand and a stick in the other. Felix watched as the woman began to beat the rug, hard, sending little puffs of dirt into the air.

Maisie shoved him forward.

"Hey," he said.

The woman stopped beating the rug and turned sharply in their direction.

"Where in the world have you two come from?" she said.

"We've been at sea," Maisie told her.

"You poor things! In what country did you find those terrible clothes?"

Maisie looked down at her jeans and fleece vest. "The colonies," she answered.

The woman *tsked*.

"We're looking for Alexander," Maisie said. "Hamilton?"

"He's already down at Beekman and Cruger," the woman said. "There's an auction today, and he had to get ready."

Felix had gone to an auction once with their mother. Some rich person had died and all of her belongings were up for sale. Fancy clocks and ornate silverware, china and ugly paintings, carpets and jewelry. The auctioneer had talked very quickly, so quickly that every time he spoke, Felix had giggled.

"Can kids go to the auction, too?" Felix asked the woman.

"Most everyone does," the woman said.

She rolled the rug up and stuck it under her arm. But instead of going back inside, she stared at Maisie and Felix a bit longer.

"Would you children like some breakfast?" she asked finally.

"Yes!" Maisie said.

"Please!" Felix added.

"Come inside then," she said.

Without hesitating, Maisie and Felix did just that.

$

After eating eggs and fried bread and bananas, Maisie and Felix made their way back to King's Street and Beekman and Cruger.

"I wonder if there's pirate booty for auction," Felix said.

"Doubloons!" Maisie said.

"Rubies!"

"Swords!"

Excited, they entered the building with the number 56-57 on it. Just like the day before, the large main room was empty. But from outside behind the store, they heard shouting and cheering. At the door that led out there, all they could see was a thick sea of people.

"It's already so crowded," Maisie said. "They must have really great stuff."

As soon as they stepped out into the yard, they paused, confused.

More than two hundred black men huddled there. Their ribs jutted out from hunger, and their bodies had oozing lesions everywhere. Some men had dried blood on their backs or cheeks. Some had swollen eyes or lips. Burn marks from ropes circled their ankles and wrists.

"What the heck?" Maisie whispered.

A group of white men stood among them, rubbing their skin with oil until it shone in the hot sun.

Once the black men had their skin oiled, they took up hot irons and curled one another's hair, braiding it with ropes.

"A good lot," a man standing in front of Maisie and Felix said.

They recognized him from last night. He'd taken them to the Stevenses' house.

"Prime slaves, they are," he added.

"Slaves!" Maisie blurted. "You mean they're auctioning men?"

The people around her laughed.

"*Men?* Hardly," someone scoffed.

"These slaves have come from the Gold Coast and won't even go for thirty pounds," someone else said.

"A good mule costs more than one of these," the man said, sending everyone into laughter again.

"You can't have slaves!" Maisie shouted. "It's immoral! These are human beings, you know, you can't—"

A strong hand clapped over her mouth from behind, silencing her. Another hand gripped her arm and dragged her, kicking, out of the yard and into the store.

Once inside, she was released. She spun around and found Alexander Hamilton standing there.

"Are you a slave trader?" she demanded.

"My boss Cruger is," he said.

"But you must stop it. Did you see how sick

those men are? How hungry?"

Alexander set his violet-blue eyes on her, his face solemn.

"Don't you think I know that?" he said quietly. "I live here. I see how these poor men have to live and the work they have to do, while the rich men sit in their fancy houses on their mahogany chairs, eating French cheeses and drinking French wine. But Nicholas Cruger is my employer. And I need this job."

Maisie remembered what the man had told them last night. Alexander was an orphan, alone in the world.

"Still," she said.

"Saint Croix is a neutral Danish port," he continued. "Cargo can move through here without fussing with British laws, which tax everything that passes through there."

"Cargo?" Maisie said. "They're human beings. They have mothers and fathers and . . ." She stopped herself. "I'm sorry," she said. "I know that your mother died."

"What of it?" he asked angrily. "Do you believe that being an orphan dictates my life? That I'll be sitting here on that stool forever?"

"I just meant—"

"You just need to mind your own business," he said. "And keep your mouth shut with all your opinions about how things should work here."

With that, he stormed off.

CHAPTER 7

The *Royal Danish-American Gazette*

"I hate Alexander Hamilton," Maisie said when Felix met her outside Beekman and Cruger.

"Sure you do," Felix said. He felt queasy after what he'd just seen. Of course he knew that people used to own slaves. He knew they treated slaves brutally. But he had never imagined anything like what he had witnessed out back.

"You okay?" Maisie asked gently. "You're pale."

Tears welled up in Felix's eyes. "I can't stand how people treated one another," he managed to say.

"It's terrible," Maisie said, wrapping her arm around her brother.

"I want to go home," Felix said through his tears.

"We are. There's a ship tomorrow, and we're going to be on it."

Felix freed himself from her grasp. "No!" he said. "I want to go back to Newport. I want it to be the twenty-first century, and I want Mom making dinner and you across the hall on the computer—"

"And Dad across the world in Doha?" Maisie said.

Felix took a deep breath. "I don't want that, but that's how it is, Maisie. And we have to get used to it."

"Used to it?" Maisie said angrily. "I'll never get used to it! I don't want Mom and Dad to be divorced. I hate it!"

Now Maisie was crying, and it was Felix's turn to comfort her.

"I'm not saying I like it," he said softly as he patted her back. "I'm just saying we have to accept it."

"No!" Maisie said even more adamantly than before.

A shadow fell across them.

"What's wrong this time?" Alexander Hamilton said.

Maisie glared at him. "Get lost!" she said. "You're . . . you're . . . disgusting!!"

Alexander grinned. "Quite a temper on this one," he said to Felix.

"Nothing is fair," Maisie cried. "Not what's going on out back or what's going on in my family."

Alexander's face grew serious. "You're right," he said. "But it's our job to not be defeated by injustice. I got angry at you back there because you showed me sympathy. If I spent every day being pitied and feeling sorry for myself, I would never get to New York to study."

Maisie wiped her eyes and nodded.

"I intend to change the world," Alexander said.

"How are you going to do that?" Maisie said.

"I don't know yet," he admitted. "Maybe become a physician like Neddy. Maybe by writing great things. I still have so much more learning to do. I've read most of Plutarch and Pope, and of course Virgil and Horace, but I'm desperate to read everything."

From down King's Street came a voice calling, "Alexander! Alexander Hamilton!"

"That's Reverend Knox," Alexander explained.

"Here!" he called to the man.

"Ah!" Reverend Knox said. He waved a newspaper as he neared. "They printed your letter about the hurricane and how it devastated our island, Alexander! And already all of Christiansted is talking about it." The reverend, a tall man with severe posture, spoke with a thick Scottish accent. "You must come with me to my office. Everyone is gathered there, and they want to see you."

Alexander's eyes sparkled. "This could be it, Reverend," he said. "What I've been waiting for."

Reverend Knox stood in front of them now, nodding. "You need to leave the islands, son," he said, "in order to get the education you deserve. This could be your ticket to the colonies."

He handed Alexander the newspaper, which he had open to the page with the letter printed on it.

As Alexander read, Maisie and Felix peered over his shoulder, reading along with him.

"I appreciate your introduction to my letter," Alexander said.

"All true," the reverend said.

Even though the letter was about the hurricane that had hit Saint Croix two months earlier, the language Alexander used was so overdramatic that Maisie had to try hard not to laugh. It was all *dost thou* and *vile* this and *vile* that, with lots of exclamation points, which her teacher back home, Mrs. Witherspoon, said were the sign of a bad writer.

But when Alexander looked up from the newspaper, he was clearly moved.

"My gratitude—" he began.

"Nonsense!" Reverend Knox said, holding up his hand as if to stop Alexander's apology.

Alexander clutched the reverend's hand in his own, and the older man took him into an embrace.

When they parted, Alexander turned to Maisie.

"Did you read it?" he asked her.

"Yes," she lied.

"Then you saw the final line? *Ye who revel in affluence?* You see now that I am aware of this gap?"

Felix had read the whole thing and was totally impressed by it. Sure, the language was old-fashioned and even flowery, but he could recognize how well written the piece was and how passionate Alexander felt. "Yes!" he said. "It's wonderful!"

"Thank you," Alexander said, keeping his eyes on Maisie.

"My teacher said exclamation points are a sign of a bad writer," Maisie blurted.

Alexander and the reverend burst into laughter.

"Who is this child?" Reverend Knox asked.

"Maisie Robbins," Maisie said. "And I'm not a child. I'm almost thirteen"

The reverend laughed again. "That would make you twelve then, wouldn't it?"

"They've come from the colonies," Alexander explained. "Rhode Island."

"Rhode Island," the reverend said, nodding. "I did my undergraduate studies at Yale, in Connecticut, and my postgraduate at the College of New Jersey. And I lived in Delaware for a time. So tell me, how are things in the colonies?"

He asked the question with a somber tone.

"Things are . . . fine," Felix said.

Alexander and the reverend exchanged a confused look.

"The Loyalists aren't causing trouble for the Colonists?" Reverend Knox asked.

"Well . . . ," Felix said, thinking hard.

Of course! The Revolutionary War hadn't even begun yet. No Boston Tea Party. No Shot Heard Round the World.

"Of course there are some very unhappy people," Felix added.

Maisie looked at him, confused.

"Unhappy with the king," he added.

"Yes, we've heard," Reverend Knox said. He turned to Alexander. "Shall we go to my office?"

"Yes," Alexander said. "My heavens, yes!"

The two men put their arms around each other's shoulders and started to walk off.

"Come on," Maisie said to Felix.

"Come on where?"

"Wherever they're going," she said.

Maisie and Felix crouched outside under the open window of Reverend Knox's office, a room off his peach-colored house. The office was full of men who smoked cigars and drank and talked excitedly to one another in booming voices.

Finally one of them called for silence.

"We are here to deliver our good news to young Mr. Hamilton," someone said.

"Here, here!" the others shouted, clinking their spoons against their glasses.

Then the crowd grew quiet.

"Alexander," a man said in a somber tone.

Maisie recognized Alexander's voice as he answered, "Mr. Kortwright."

"Your employer and my associate, the esteemed Nicholas Cruger, and I have come to an agreement this afternoon after reading your letter in the *Gazette*."

Mr. Kortwright paused for what seemed to be forever. Maisie found herself holding her breath as she waited for him to speak again.

Finally he said, "We've gathered the men you see here today, men who have witnessed firsthand your good business sense and keen intelligence in the absence of Mr. Cruger during his illness this past year, men who have read your literary writings, men who, as the merchants and leaders of this fine island, believe in you, young Mr. Hamilton. Men who believe that you should have the opportunity to pursue your studies in New York."

Maisie gasped. "He's going to New York," she whispered. "He is the one we're supposed to meet and give the coin to."

"I think you're right," Felix whispered back.

Again, Mr. Kortwright had paused dramatically.

"Therefore," he continued at last, "Nicholas Cruger has agreed to consign four annual cargoes of Saint Croix produce to be sold toward your support and education."

Reverend Knox spoke then. "Alexander," he said, his voice softer than Mr. Kortwright's, "we have secured contributions from all of the men you see here in this room. The four hundred pounds of pledges will cover four years of tuition and board as well as your transportation to the mainland. Letters of recommendation have been written to our close friends and associates, who we trust will welcome you into their homes and guide you."

"My gratitude—" Alexander began, but he was immediately hushed.

"Your potential, my dear boy," Reverend Knox said, "is limitless."

"I suspect you will soon be with my son Neddy," a new voice said, "taking premedical studies."

"Then on to Edinburgh," Reverend Knox added.

Alexander laughed. "Let me first get into a college, Reverend."

"There is only one obstacle," Nicholas Cruger said seriously. "The American school year has already started, and there is only one more safe sailing there before winter arrives."

"Why is this a problem?" Alexander asked.

"The ship sails tonight," Cruger said. "It leaves

in a matter of hours."

Maisie grabbed Felix's hand and held on tight.

"Well then," Alexander said. "I need to go and pack."

Everyone in the room burst into wild applause.

"I will meet you on the dock," Reverend Knox said above the din. "I have your ticket to Boston, and then a stagecoach ticket on to New York."

Maisie gasped. She turned to her brother and said, "That's it, Felix! We have to get on that ship!"

CHAPTER 8

Stowaways

As Maisie and Felix ran down to the dock, Felix began to worry.

"What about pirates?" he asked his sister. "What about shipwrecks?"

"We'll worry about all that once we get on that ship," Maisie said without slowing down.

"But we don't have any money for tickets," Felix said, struggling to keep up.

At that, Maisie stopped. "I know," she said, grinning. "We're going to stow away."

"What? No way!" Felix said. He folded his arms across his chest to show her he meant it.

"People do it all the time," Maisie said.

"Like who?" Felix said, exasperated.

"Like . . . like . . . stowaways," she said, and with that she took off again toward the docks.

"That's a ridiculous answer!" Felix called after her.

When she didn't even pause, Felix started off after her, his chest heavy with worry. Even if he could put aside his fears about the catastrophes that might happen at sea, now that the ships were coming into view, he couldn't ignore the fact that the only time he ever went on a sailboat, he threw up the entire afternoon.

Old friends of his parents had invited them to their beach house in Connecticut. The weekend had been boring, full of private jokes between his parents and the other couple, late-night dinners of food Felix didn't like—leg of lamb and swordfish and lots of zucchini—and the couple's baby screaming all the time. Worse, they'd spent that Saturday on a sailboat, a Pearson, the guy had said all braggy—and Felix threw up as soon as they left the dock. He didn't stop until they got back three hours later. *Keep your eye on the horizon*, the guy kept telling him. But if you're seasick and the world is spinning, how are you supposed to do that?

"Maisie," Felix said, already queasy with anticipation, "remember Connecticut? Remember the Pearson?"

The night was the blackest night he had ever seen, despite the stars glittering high above them. Just the sound of the waves crashing against the docks made him queasy. Felix wondered if he'd ever wanted his own bed more than he did standing there in the darkness.

Maisie stood surveying the ships as if she could figure out which one was headed to Boston.

"Yeah, I remember the Pearson," she said. "That crabby baby. Talullah."

"And me throwing up. Remember?"

She turned to him, her eyes clouding with the memory. "Felix," she said, grabbing both his shoulders firmly, "you have to keep your eye on the horizon. You have to get through this."

"Are you kidding? For like a month?"

Maisie considered this. "You have to," she said finally. "Now let's find that ship."

Felix watched his sister walk purposefully down the dock and right up to a group of sailors heaving barrels onto a ship. Slowly, he joined her there.

A burly sailor with a red beard and a nose shaped like a turnip pointed toward a large five-masted ship. "The *Thunderbolt*'s the one, Missy. She's sailing to America."

Hearing the name *Thunderbolt* made Felix's stomach jump nervously. He hadn't even considered thunder out there yet.

"Thank you, sir," Maisie said in the sweetest voice she could muster. She practically skipped off, tugging Felix's hand for him to follow.

"*Thunderbolt?*" he moaned. "We really need to rethink this idea."

"*Thunderbolt,*" Maisie said. "It sounds fast, right? We'll be in Boston in no time."

$

Maisie couldn't believe how easy it was to sneak onto the ship. No one even seemed to notice the two of them as they walked on board. No one came around collecting tickets or asking where they belonged. They just slipped by, unnoticed.

"I don't like this one bit," Felix said.

Maisie decided to ignore him. She'd gotten all worried when they'd landed in Clara Barton's barn because of the way he'd carried on about his arm, which he was convinced he'd broken. In the end, all he had was a big bruise on his elbow. If she let him, he'd talk himself into being seasick before they'd even set sail. No, Maisie thought, she would have to convince him that he would be just fine.

"I read somewhere that seasickness is unusually rare on large ships," Maisie said. From the ship's railing, she kept her eye on the passengers boarding the ship, watching for Alexander to show up.

"Really?" Felix said, squinting suspiciously at her.

"Yup," she said.

Maisie saw Alexander's small body lugging a heavy trunk onto the dock. Several wealthy-looking men accompanied him, one of them talking and gesturing wildly, another carrying a small suitcase, and yet another helping push the trunk. She considered waving to him but thought better of it. Probably not a good idea to draw attention to themselves until the ship had set sail.

"Maybe we should go below? Kind of hide?" Felix suggested as if he'd read her mind.

"Good idea," Maisie agreed.

They followed the stream of people disappearing down steps that led below deck. The stairs were rickety wooden things that seemed to go on forever. Finally, they reached the lower deck. It smelled like sweat and food she didn't want to eat. The ceiling was low and the halls narrow, giving Maisie a claustrophobic feeling. *It would be easy to get seasick down here,* she thought.

"Once we leave the harbor, we'll go back up," she told her brother. "So you can look at the horizon."

Panic swept across Felix's face. "What if it rains? What if it lightnings? I can't stay up there. And it's awful down here. It's smelly and close and dark."

Maisie thought fast. "Maybe Alexander will let us stay with him in his cabin," she said. "I bet that'll be better than this."

"Why would he ever do that?" Felix said, exasperated.

"Because he'll take pity on us," Maisie said with more certainty than she felt.

"But what if—"

Maisie sighed, loud and dramatic. "Can we please just take it one step at a time?"

More passengers came down the stairs now, into the large area where Maisie and Felix stood. They pushed past them on their way to their cabins. Men carried trunks on their shoulders, and women had large square baskets in their hands. The ship rocked from all the movement, and Felix placed his hand on the wall to steady himself.

A woman in a blue hat with a feather in it paused in front of Maisie.

"Are you turned around?" she asked in an Irish accent.

"Uh . . . yes," Maisie said.

"Confusing, isn't it?" the woman said, and moved on.

A bell clanged above them, and excited voices filtered down.

"I think we're taking off," Maisie said, excited herself.

"Maisie Robbins?" a voice said.

Maisie followed it and saw Alexander making his way toward her through the other passengers. His reddish hair stuck up at funny angles in the heat like her own did, and he was grinning.

"You're on this ship, too?" he said, pleased.

Maisie nodded.

"Which cabin are you in?" Alexander said, taking

a slip of paper from his pocket and checking his own ticket.

Just then the ship lurched forward. People on deck clapped and shouted. The sound of sails being raised and catching the wind filled the ship as the *Thunderbolt* moved quickly away from the island of Saint Croix.

"The funny thing is," Maisie said, "we actually don't have tickets."

$

Alexander closed the door of his cabin after Maisie and Felix settled themselves inside. They sat side by side on the small sofa, Felix practically not breathing at all in anticipation of what Alexander might do with them.

"Explain yourselves, please," Alexander said quietly, leveling his blue eyes directly at them.

"Well," Maisie began.

When she didn't say anything more, Alexander said, "Yes?"

"Well," Maisie said again, nodding this time. "We need to get back to New York, but we're out of money."

Felix nodded, too. "That's the exact truth," he said.

"Please don't turn us in," Maisie said.

"Do you see that trunk?" Alexander said, pointing to a scuffed brown leather trunk. "It's filled with books. Books I need to read on this journey. When I arrive in New York, I need to catch up so that I can go to King's College and complete my studies. I'm about as behind as a person can be."

"We won't bother you," Maisie said. "We promise. You can read the entire time, and you won't even know we're here."

Alexander began to pace.

"Surely I wouldn't be on this ship if it weren't for the kindness of others," he said.

Even though he spoke out loud, it was clear he was speaking to himself. "Ever since Mother died, I've had to rely on my own good intuition and ambition and intelligence, and that has gotten me where I am right now," he continued, still pacing. "Aren't these letters of recommendation in my pocket from men who believe in me? Wouldn't I be completely rudderless without Reverend Knox or Mr. Stevens or even Mr. Cruger to guide me?"

Alexander stopped pacing and looked at Maisie and Felix.

"Yes," he said. "You'll stay here in my cabin. Out of my way, quiet as mice."

Maisie jumped up. "Thank you so much!" she said.

"But if anything happens, like what happened to the *Halcyon* two weeks ago, you'll have to look out for yourselves," he said.

Felix got up, too, but slowly. "Wh-what happened to the *Halcyon*?" he asked.

"Pirates," Alexander said. "On this very route."

"Pirates!" Felix said, glaring at Maisie.

The truth was, the idea of pirates seemed exciting to Maisie. She imagined handsome men in white ruffled shirts and big black hats with skulls and crossbones on them rushing the ship. Swords slashing through the air. Maybe one of them would have a wooden leg. Maybe one of them would have a parrot on his shoulder.

"These are dangerous seas," Alexander said.

Still caught up in her fantasy, Maisie just shrugged.

But Felix asked, "What happened to the *Halcyon's* passengers?"

"Murdered, of course," Alexander said.

$

The journey from Saint Croix to Boston would take almost three weeks. Alexander brought them bread from dinner and fruit, and sometimes molasses cake that tasted terrible. Felix spent much of his time on deck, keeping his eye on the horizon and on the lookout for pirates. He wasn't sure what to look for exactly, but he hoped he would recognize them if they appeared. To his surprise, he didn't get seasick that first week. He enjoyed the spray of salt water that misted his face and the occasional glimpse he caught of dolphins leaping into the air. Once he saw three whales, breaching and spouting water from their blowholes. At night, he liked to lie on his back and gaze up at the inky sky with its seemingly endless stars twinkling at him.

One night, Alexander joined him up there. He brought Felix some dried cod that was salty and fishy but somehow tasted delicious.

"Do you see Orion there?" Alexander said, tracing the outline of the hunter and his belt with his fingers.

"I do!" Felix said. Back home, lights blocked out the stars. Even in Newport, he couldn't really make out the shapes of constellations. But here, the stars arranged themselves so clearly in the sky that he could almost imagine Orion hunting up there.

"Cassiopeia," Alexander said, this time tracing the shape of the three sisters. "Ah!" he said. "Look at the Big Dipper."

"Like a ladle," Felix said. "Scooping up the ocean."

"You must be a poet, too," Alexander said.

"Oh, I don't know." Felix had never admitted to anyone that indeed he did like to write poems. "Do you know what a haiku is?" he asked Alexander.

"Is it a poem of some kind?"

"Yes. Three lines. Five syllables in the first line. Seven in the second. And then five again in the third," Felix explained. "I like to write those. My teacher last year hung mine up on the bulletin board."

"Did she?" Alexander said, impressed. "Can you recite it for me?"

"I think so," Felix said, even though of course he could recite it. He knew it by heart and could picture it, printed in dark blue ink, the paper mounted on lighter blue construction paper, hanging there for the whole school to see.

Felix cleared his throat. "Why does love vanish? Just yesterday we smiled. Today our hearts break."

"Bravo," Alexander said softly. "I counted the syllables as you spoke. Such an interesting form."

"It's Japanese," Felix said. Saying the poem had made him suddenly sad, remembering how he'd written it after his parents told them they were getting divorced. Remembering how his heart did break that day.

"Japanese?" Alexander said, puzzled.

Was Japan not a country in 1772? Felix wondered. *Or maybe it was called something else back then?*

"Near China?" he tried.

"Ah," Alexander said. "The Orient."

The moon was full but waxing. Beside it, a small, bright star blazed.

"Can you recite one of yours?" Felix asked.

Alexander was quick to agree. "Ah! Whither, whither am I flown, A wandering guest in worlds unknown?"

Tears sprang to Felix's eyes. "It's as if you've written that for me and Maisie," he said.

"Truly? Are you two wandering guests in worlds unknown?" Alexander asked.

Felix gazed up at all the stars.

"You have no idea," he said, sighing.

CHAPTER 9

The *Thunderbolt*

After a week at sea, a routine had developed in Alexander's cabin. He slept and studied in the room with the bed, and Maisie and Felix took turns sleeping on the couch in the sitting room. Alexander had requested extra blankets so that the one sleeping on the floor could be more comfortable. Felix had borrowed some books from Alexander, and he was content to curl up and read or sit up on the deck. But Maisie was growing restless. Even though Alexander was conceited, a know-it-all, and more confident than anyone she'd ever known, she had to admit—to herself—that she'd developed a crush on the short, redheaded seventeen-year-old.

By the end of the second week, she became

determined to get him to pay attention to her. She couldn't do it by talking about poetry, like Felix did. Or computer games, movies, TV shows, or any of the things that made up her world. No, the only thing she had that Alexander was interested in, Maisie decided, was her knowledge of New York.

On their sixteenth day at sea, Maisie finally had her chance. Felix was up on the deck, and when Alexander came back from lunch with their smuggled bread and butter, Maisie was waiting for him. She'd wet her hair and combed it with her fingers, trying to tame it as best she could in such damp air. Alexander walked in and as usual, hardly looked at her.

"Here you are," he said, placing a large linen napkin on the small table by the couch. He unfolded it to reveal the thick slabs of bread smeared with butter. From his pocket he took out two oranges.

"Oh," Maisie said, "I love oranges."

"Mmmm," Alexander said, already lost in thought.

Maisie remembered how her father, who had grown up in New Jersey, had told her that when his grandfather was young, oranges were a rare treat.

Sometimes he got an orange in his Christmas stocking, her father had said. Maisie had thought that was just about the worst thing to find in your Christmas stocking. She always got gel pens, purple Post-its, holiday-flavored Lip Smackers, a deck of cards, butterfly clips and bands for her hair, Sour Patch Kids, piña colada–flavored gum . . . thinking of her Christmas stocking, with her name written across the top in gold glitter made her too sad. *What would we do this Christmas?* she wondered suddenly. Their first one without their father.

She forgot all about oranges and her plan to warn Alexander about how scarce they were in New York (because if her grandfather couldn't always get them in the 1940s, no way would they be all over New York in 1772).

"Did you say something?" Alexander asked her.

Maisie shook her head. She hadn't said anything. She'd sniffled.

He shrugged and picked up a book, heading into the bedroom with it.

"I was thinking about Christmas," Maisie said.

Alexander stopped and turned to her. "Christmas? Why?"

"It's my first one without my father," she said quietly.

"He isn't in New York?"

She shook her head.

"I see," Alexander said.

He looked as if he might walk into the bedroom, but then thought better of it. Instead, he sat in the big leather chair across from the couch.

"It is difficult," Alexander said. "To be without your parent."

Maisie realized that he must think her father had died. His own mother had, and his father had deserted him. Actually, Alexander was a good person to talk about this with.

"He lives in . . ." Maisie tried to think. Qatar probably wasn't a country yet. "The Middle East," she said finally.

"Forever?"

"I'm afraid so. He and my mother got divorced," she explained.

Alexander nodded thoughtfully. "My mother had complicated relationships, too," he said. "Does he write to you?" he asked.

"No, he . . ." Maisie almost said "calls once a week"

but stopped herself. No telephones, she remembered.

"Neither does mine," Alexander said. His violet eyes looked at her as if he were seeing her for the first time. "After Mother died, I thought he might come to Saint Croix and take me with him. But he didn't."

"Where does he live?"

"From what I understand, he moves from island to island. Following work."

"My father is supposed to come to Newport for Christmas," Maisie said. She hadn't considered that he might not come, but hearing Alexander made her worry.

"But he's working at this new museum, acquiring art and setting up galleries and stuff, and what if they don't let him leave? I liked it better when he was just a painter and lived with us."

When she said this, Maisie could picture her father in his paint-splattered clothes, riding his bike home from his studio. She could remember how happy she used to get when she saw him coming up Hudson Street, how she would run down the block to meet him. His hugs smelled of turpentine and oil paint and were a little sweaty.

"Do you miss him?" Maisie asked.

"Yes. I write him every week," Alexander said. His pale skin seemed even paler when he added, "I worry about him. Last year, I read in the *Gazette* that his house was attacked during a slave uprising in Tobago. My father was shot in the thigh—"

"What?" Maisie gasped.

"It could have been worse," Alexander said solemnly. "Two men were killed. Still, I wrote him, so full of worry that I could hardly sleep. But he didn't answer my letters."

"Is he all right?" Maisie asked, still horrified.

"I have heard he recovered and is living on Saint Kitts."

Alexander looked so sad that Maisie reached over and put her hand on his. To her surprise, he did not recoil. A funny feeling ran through her, and she pulled her hand back. Although Maisie had never had a crush before, she had once considered developing one on Tripp Truitt. Tripp was a grade ahead of her, and everybody had a crush on him because he was tall and his bangs fell in his eyes in an adorable way and he rode a skateboard to school.

Yes, Maisie thought as she considered Alexander Hamilton, even though the whole school knew that

Tripp Truitt was crush worthy, she had decided against wasting her time on him. So why in the world was this short, pale, redhead with the giant ego making her feel this way? Why couldn't she have crushes on the right boys?

"Don't be upset," Alexander said. "I'm sure you will see your father at Christmas. Why, he must already be sailing toward America to make it there in time!"

"I hope so," Maisie said.

"If you want to talk more about this . . . ," Alexander said as he stood.

"Thank you," Maisie said.

He smiled at her, and her stomach did a little flip.

"For everything," she added.

"I am delighted to help," he said.

"If you ever want to know more about New York, I can tell you about it. I lived there my whole life until just a couple of months ago."

"We shall make time for that conversation," he said. "But for now, I need to study."

Maisie watched him as he walked across the sitting room and into the bedroom. In no time, she heard him talking to himself in there. Maisie grinned. That was how he studied. He paced back and forth, talking out loud to himself. *Alexander Hamilton*, she thought. For a moment she remembered Clara Barton—how she had grown up to create the American Red Cross and nurse soldiers in the Civil War and all sorts of awesome things. What, she wondered now, would Alexander Hamilton do when he grew up?

$

After more than two weeks at sea, boredom struck. The *Thunderbolt* hit some rainy weather, so they couldn't sit up on the deck. Felix started to worry again about getting seasick. To distract him, Maisie asked Alexander for some paper and a pen so they could play the dots game. They had spent hours playing this game when it rained and they were stuck in the apartment on Bethune Street. They would take turns drawing a line to connect two dots, and when the line completed a square, they got to write their initials in it. The one with the most squares at the end won.

Of course, the pen now was a quill that she had to dip into an inkwell, which was pretty messy. Maisie kept dripping ink all over the paper and herself, until her fingers were stained. But eventually she got the hang of it, and she presented Felix with the game all set up, the paper covered with dots.

Felix, who had even grown bored with writing poetry, whooped when he saw the game.

Happily, Felix took the quill and connected his first two dots.

"This is nice," he said.

"See? And you haven't gotten seasick," Maisie said, dipping the quill in the ink and connecting two dots.

"Don't jinx it," Felix said, only half kidding. "We're not there yet."

No sooner did the words leave Felix's mouth than the ship, without any warning, leaned hard to the right, sending Felix tumbling off the sofa.

Felix screamed. Images from the *Titanic* movie flashed across his mind. The night his family rented it, he'd had nightmares.

Maisie and the chair slid smack into the bedroom door.

But before either of them could get to their feet, the ship heaved to the left. Felix rolled to the other end, screaming, "Help!" the entire way.

This time Maisie got thrown from the chair and landed in a heap beside her brother.

The bedroom door flew open, slamming hard against the wall. Maisie caught a glimpse of Alexander, both hands on the wall for balance, moving slowly toward them.

"A storm," he managed to say before—once again—the *Thunderbolt* sent Maisie and Felix across the floor.

"We're all going to die!" Felix cried.

From the small window in the sitting room, they saw flashes of lightning. The rain, which had been falling steadily for several days now, pounded the window. From the hall outside the room came the sound of people running and shouting.

The ship rocked, back and forth, as if it, too, were trying to find its balance.

"Alexander!" Maisie yelled above the din. "Should we go on deck?" As afraid as she was, somehow she felt safer with him in charge.

"Stay here until I find out what's going on," he said.

From the floor, she watched as he fought gravity, pulling himself across the room and out the door.

Felix grabbed hold of the legs of the desk and held on tight.

"Oh," he said over and over. "Oh, oh, oh, oh."

For a few minutes, the only sounds were Felix's whimpering, the rain hitting the window hard, the crack of thunder, and the occasional electric zap of lightning, which would light the dark blue sky.

Then Maisie laughed.

"Are you crazy?" Felix managed to ask her.

"No," she said. "But I'm sure we're not going to die."

The boat took its hardest pitch yet and Felix's oh came out like a moan from a horror movie.

Maisie laughed again. "Calm down," she said in a perfectly normal voice. "This ship is not going to sink because Alexander Hamilton is on it. Obviously he makes it to New York and goes on to do whatever it is he goes on to do."

"Right," Felix said, trying to get his hands and legs to stop shaking. "But we don't know if the ship actually sinks, and he manages to survive. We don't know if maybe he floated around in the ocean for days waiting to be rescued. Maybe . . ."

He stopped himself. The possibilities were too

terrifying to say out loud. Once again visions of the *Titanic* movie popped into his head, this time ones from *after* it sunk.

"Oh," Felix whimpered.

The door creaked open, and Alexander came back inside the cabin.

"It's a pretty bad storm," he said, holding on to the doorframe. "I think we should ride it out down here."

"Do—do—they think we're going to sink?" Felix stammered.

"We just have to ride the storm out," Alexander said firmly.

"We will," Maisie said.

"Oh," Felix moaned as the ship lurched yet again.

$

"I told you so," Maisie whispered to Felix when the storm finally ended the next day. All night they had rolled and swayed in the cabin, holding on to the edges of whatever they sat or laid on. Alexander managed to bring them some broth from the dining room where, he reported, glasses and dishes were breaking with regularity.

"Well, excuse me for not wanting to get

shipwrecked or lost at sea or . . ." Once again he stopped himself. Even though they had survived the storm, what might have happened still had him trembling.

Maisie picked up the dot game. "Now," she said, "where were we?"

From outside their cabin, hurried footsteps pounded down the corridor. The sound of people shouting filled the air.

"Now what?" Maisie groaned.

This time, the cabin door burst open and Alexander stood there, his eyes wild and a look of terror on his face.

"Hurry!" he ordered them. "On deck!"

Felix and Maisie jumped up.

Alexander turned and motioned for them to follow.

"What's going on?" Maisie asked him.

Without turning around he answered, "The ship is on fire. We need to evacuate. Now."

CHAPTER 10

Fire!

"On fire?" Maisie shouted.

She thought about the nice, orderly fire drills at school: the special exit they used, the buddy they walked out with, how they waited—bored—until the principal announced they could return to their classrooms. But this was a real fire. And they were not able to exit at sea. Her heart pounded. Not with fear, though. With excitement. They had survived the storm, and Maisie knew they would survive the fire, too.

"Follow me," Alexander ordered. "All passengers need to be on deck in case—"

"We sink?" Felix squeaked.

"Yes," Alexander said firmly. "In case we sink."

Maisie left the cabin quickly, wondering what she would see out there. But Felix stayed put as if he were frozen in place.

"Come now, Felix," Alexander said in a no-nonsense voice. "No time for tears or fears."

Felix nodded and forced his legs to move forward. They felt like they were made of lead. His whole body felt that way. Sometimes Felix dreamed he was being chased, and his legs seemed unable to cooperate, heavy and stiff. Like now. But this was no dream. It was really happening. As he made his slow way to the door, he heard frightened screams from above and men shouting orders and saw women clutching their children's hands and running down the hall right in front of him, asking, "What's happening? What's happening?"

Alexander pushed his way through the crowd to go and help on deck. By the time Felix and Maisie reached the stairs, they had become part of a large group, huddled close together and moving as if all the bodies were one being. The air hung close and reeked of smoke.

Someone at the top of the stairs shouted down to them, "Cover your nose and mouth!"

A wave of panic shuddered through the crowd as people brought their hands to their mouths, still pushing forward.

Finally Felix felt the stairs beneath his feet. From behind he was lifted up, the crowd now almost in a frenzy.

It seemed as if the stairs went straight to heaven, disappearing into what seemed like billowing clouds. But moving upward, Felix realized that the clouds were actually thickening smoke. His eyes started to sting as he moved up the smoky staircase. At the top, the smell of things burning and the flames and smoke scorched his nose and throat. A hand grabbed hold of his arm and tugged him through the smoke and into a clearer area across the deck.

"Stay here," Alexander said to him, letting go of his grasp on Felix's arm and joining the men at the rail.

Maisie stood wide-eyed beside Felix.

"I know I said that there was nothing to be afraid of," she said. "That obviously Alexander Hamilton would survive anything. But now I'm not so sure."

Felix and Maisie stared at the hot flames leaping from the ship. They could feel the heat from the fire on their faces, and the air around them had taken on a hazy, gray quality.

Then Maisie saw something she couldn't believe. "Alexander's going overboard!" Maisie shouted.

She took off in the direction of the fire and the men at the railing, where Felix saw that Alexander was indeed climbing over.

"Stay back here!" he called after his sister. But with a sinking feeling, he knew she wouldn't listen.

He took a few tentative steps toward her, but the smoke and fire frightened him too much, and he returned to the end of the deck where most of the other women and children huddled.

As she neared, Maisie saw that Alexander wasn't the only one going overboard. Many men climbed over the railing and lowered themselves on ropes toward the sea. And, she realized, they were all holding wooden buckets.

At the railing, she peered below. A dozen or more men were swinging from ropes, just above the gray sea, filling the buckets with seawater, then handing them up the rope to the next man, who handed it to the next man, until it reached the top. Waiting men took the buckets of water and ran to douse the flames with it. She thought about fire hoses and fire hydrants and fire extinguishers and all the things that worked to put out fires in her world. These buckets of seawater seemed small and ineffective in comparison.

Maisie swallowed hard, the taste of smoke burning her tongue and throat. Would these men with their buckets be able to save the *Thunderbolt* and her passengers?

$

Hours passed.

The frantic voices of the men struggling to put out the fire mixed with the cries of babies and the sounds of the crackling flames and wood splitting. The smoke grew darker and thicker. Maisie watched, mesmerized, as the men worked, continuously filling the buckets with water and passing them up the large ship's ropes to the deck. Alexander stayed in his position about midway on the rope, hanging on until a bucket reached him, then somehow taking the bucket and passing it to the man above him while still clutching the rope. Soot and cinders covered his face and hair and hands and clothes. But the men seemed not to notice. They just kept working to get the fire under control.

Eventually Felix sat down, pressed close against the others across the deck. Beside him, a woman prayed softly. He leaned against her slightly, letting her words wash over him and comfort him as he drifted into a fitful sleep. He woke with a start, looking around confused.

Then he saw that the fire still raged. The men still struggled to put it out. And his sister still stood watching them. Dawn streaked beautiful colors across the sky. Lavenders and pinks that looked blurry in the smoky air around him, but somehow pretty just the same. He could still see the crescent moon and Venus twinkling beside it. Alexander had shown him that just the other night when they sat up here looking at the stars. Felix had thought the bright light twinkling next to the moon was a star, too. *No, no,* Alexander had told him. *She's a planet. Venus.*

The woman who had prayed during the night now handed Felix a bowl.

"Sip some broth," she told him in an accent he couldn't recognize.

The bowl, brought from below by one of the

sailors, was being passed from person to person. Usually Felix refused to share cups or spoons or anything with strangers. But cold and hungry, he took the bowl gratefully and sipped. The broth tasted delicious, like chicken soup without any of the veggies or noodles. He wanted to drink it down but knew it was meant for everyone.

Felix passed it to the next person. Then, like everybody else, he waited.

$

That afternoon, word spread across the deck that the bucket brigade had almost completely put out the fire. The passengers, all of them stinking of smoke and trembling with fear, let out a whoop of thanks. Still, the men had to continue with their bucket brigade for several more hours before the captain appeared before the crowd. His cheeks had turned bright red from the heat of the fire, and his face was smeared black with soot. He looked exhausted but joyful.

"All of you can return to your cabins and thank the lord for rescuing the *Thunderbolt*."

"Amen!" the crowd said in unison.

"I think, sir," a young, pretty woman said, "we

should thank the men who saved us as well."

This time the crowd's "Amen" was even louder.

The passengers began to disperse, moving slowly below. But Felix waited for his sister.

She finally appeared with Alexander. His shirt had ripped, and he was filthy with soot. But he grinned when he saw Felix.

"We didn't sink," he said.

"Thanks to you," Maisie told Alexander.

"Not just me," he said, even though his tone was boastful.

"What if there's another fire?" Felix asked. "How did this one even start?"

"Probably in the kitchen," Alexander said. "But there's no way to know for sure."

"All I want to do is sleep until we get to Boston," Maisie said.

Alexander's smile faded.

"Let's hope that the *Thunderbolt* can complete the journey with this much damage," he said.

Felix looked past his sister and Alexander. The *Thunderbolt* was a charred mess. Water poured onto the deck from holes left by the fire. Beyond, the Atlantic Ocean stretched, seemingly forever. After all this time at sea, Boston still seemed as far away as it had the day he and Maisie sneaked onto the ship.

$

On October 25, three weeks after it left Saint Croix, the *Thunderbolt* finally limped into Long Wharf in Boston Harbor.

Once Alexander got his trunk off the ship and he and Maisie and Felix were walking down the gangway, Maisie asked him, "Now where do we get the stagecoach to New York?"

Alexander laughed. "The next one isn't for five days," he said without slowing down.

"Five days!" Felix moaned. Ahead of him he saw crowds and hills, gorgeous fall foliage, and dozens of soldiers dressed in scarlet-red coats carrying muskets and bayonets and looking fierce. "What are we going to do here for five whole days?"

"I don't know what *you're* going to do," Alexander said. "But I need to find the *Boston Gazette*. Reverend Knox had me write a plea for help for hurricane recovery on Saint Croix, and I need to convince them to publish it."

They stood in the port city now, and for the first time, Alexander paused to take in his surroundings.

He blinked once. Then again as if he couldn't believe what he saw.

"The leaves," he managed to say. "They're . . . they're red! And yellow! And . . . orange!"

Maisie laughed. "It's autumn," she explained. "The leaves turn from green to all of these colors."

"Every autumn?" he said.

"Yup."

"Why?" he asked, stunned.

"Photosynthesis," Maisie said proudly. She didn't know how to write poetry. She didn't like to read. But she loved math and science. Last year, she'd won first place in her school's science fair. She'd made a volcano that erupted and written a report on magma and Mount Saint Helens.

"Putting together with light," Alexander said. "Photosynthesis."

"Kind of," Maisie said, nodding. "It's the way plants turn water and carbon dioxide into oxygen and sugar. During winter, there's not enough light or water for photosynthesis, so the trees live off the food they stored during the summer and the green chlorophyll disappears from the leaves, showing us yellow and orange color." She could go on forever about photosynthesis, but Felix looked so bored she stopped.

Alexander, however, had put down his trunk while Maisie talked and looked at her, impressed.

"How did you figure that out?" he asked.

"She always gets an A in science," Felix said.

"Well," Alexander said, returning his gaze to the trees in the distance, "this photosynthesis is remarkable."

From out of nowhere came the sound of angry voices. In no time, a huge crowd of men marched past them, fists in the air, shouting.

"There must be a thousand men marching," Alexander said in wonderment.

He stopped a young boy running after the crowd.

"What are they doing?" he asked.

"They're on their way to Faneuil Hall," the boy said, excited. "Haven't you seen the letters in the *Gazette*?"

"We've just arrived," Alexander explained.

"There's been trouble these past weeks," the boy said.

He was eager to keep moving toward Faneuil Hall, and seeing this, Alexander began to follow the mob, Maisie and Alexander at his side.

"With the British?" Alexander asked.

"Yes, sir," the boy said. "Even after they repealed the stamp tax, they keep adding new ones. On glass and paper and tea. The merchants are boycotting everything that comes from Britain. So now they're saying we can't choose our own governors or judges, and they've sent them over here to make sure we don't cause any more trouble."

He pointed to the harbor they were passing, where enormous British warships stood watch.

From all of the side streets, more and more people joined the angry protestors.

"They've even opened a custom's house here," the boy said. "If I were that inspector, I'd run as fast as I could. This crowd intends to catch him and tar and feather him."

Alexander Hamilton stood straighter as if it could increase his small stature.

"Well, Maisie and Felix," he said, "it appears we've arrived in Boston at just the right time."

Maisie nodded, keeping up with Alexander step for step, pulling herself up straight and tall.

But Felix gladly stayed in their shadows. He did

not want to see someone tarred and feathered, that was for sure. He thought of those Redcoats and their angry faces. The revolution was coming, he knew that for certain. He just hoped it didn't start today.

CHAPTER 11

Looking for Bethune Street

For five days, Alexander, Maisie, and Felix walked the streets of Boston, watching the British Redcoats march across the Boston Common and the colonists protest British rule. They read pamphlets pasted to tavern walls arguing for independence. Alexander's excitement over the political situation combined with his burning desire to get to New York made Maisie believe even more that he was the person they were sent to find. But what did the coin mean? How would that affect his future?

Felix wasn't so sure. In his grumpier, homesick moments, he worried that Maisie was following Alexander just because she had a crush on him. It was too easy for her to lose sight of more important things, like getting back home to Newport and seeing their mother again. "I am positive he's the one," she insisted when Felix told her they should just try to get back. "No one else has come forward, have they?" she said.

The Boston to New York stagecoach left twice a week and took seven days. Reluctantly, Alexander bought tickets for Maisie and Felix, too. Maisie had been right: He took pity on them, maybe because he had been orphaned and homeless himself. The ticket included lodging in taverns along the way. The best part of the stagecoach ride along the bumpy Post Road was those taverns where they stopped each night. The taverns all had big fireplaces with roaring fires burning in them, low ceilings, and long wooden tables. They always seemed to be crowded. Men drank beer and hard cider and passionately debated taxes and duties the British placed on items. Felix thought he could sit and listen to them all night as they explored the pros and cons of separating from British rule.

As he ate big slabs of homemade bread toasted with melted Havarti cheese or large wedges of pork pie, always followed by spice cake topped with cream, Felix wondered what life would have been like if the colonists had not fought the British. Listening to the debates swirling around him, he realized how close he came to being a British citizen. How close they all came to never having a United States at all.

Inside the stagecoach were heavy, scratchy blankets that Maisie and Felix huddled under. In all, the stagecoach held eight passengers, all of them grown men except for Maisie, Felix, and Alexander. The leaves had started to fall from the trees, and every night there was frost. The week on the road, though boring and uncomfortable, lulled her. Every now and then, she would sigh and tell Felix that she wished something exciting would happen, but overall she was content to stare out the window at the beautiful Connecticut landscape. And to sneak glances at Alexander Hamilton, who had become by now a full-fledged crush.

Sitting across from him in the stagecoach, she watched the ways his eyes shone when he talked to the other passengers. Even though he was thin and short, he had the confidence of someone as tall as a skyscraper. His energy and curiosity seemed endless. He wanted to know exactly where they were, what lay ahead, how the other people felt about British rule. He commented with such intelligence that Maisie fell under a spell listening to him.

When the stagecoach driver stuck his head in the carriage after a stop one morning and announced they would arrive on Manhattan Island by noon, Maisie grew sad that the journey was ending. Not that Alexander paid her much attention. She tried to add her opinion to the conversations, but she could see that he considered her a little girl. More than once she found herself wishing she were at least thirteen because it sounded so much better than twelve.

Felix was surprised how his sister hung on every word Alexander had to say about everything. When their old school held a mock presidential election, Maisie never cast her vote. *Who cares?* she'd said. *It's only make-believe!* Now here she was asking questions about King George and trying to put in her two cents about it all. Felix sighed watching her watch Alexander. All they had to do was give him that coin, find Bethune Street, and then get back to

Newport. He was more than ready for his own bed.

The stagecoach slowed as it entered Manhattan, and Felix peered out the window. This was Manhattan, but it did not look at all familiar. The streets were lined with trees, and a small brick church stood at the end of one. A large grassy area with an even larger flagpole in the middle reminded Felix of Boston Common, where they had watched John Hancock march in the parade last week. But he knew there was no such place in New York City.

He nudged his sister. "Where are we?" he whispered.

Maisie stared out the window, too, puzzled. "In Tribeca, I think."

Tribeca was where city hall and the courthouse stood. And where their father's studio used to be, off North Moore Street. It felt weird to be in Manhattan and not see any of these familiar landmarks.

The man sitting beside Alexander pointed out the window.

"That's Liberty Pole," he said, "sitting on Bowling Green. The Redcoats tried to blow her up a few years back, but she refused to go down. You heard of the Battle of Golden Hill?"

"No," Maisie answered, even though he wasn't talking to her.

The man ignored her and kept talking to Alexander. "The Sons of Liberty went at it in the wheat field up the street with a few dozen British soldiers. A lot of men were hurt that night," he said sadly. "These are dangerous times, young man."

The stagecoach came to a stop.

"Where to now?" Maisie asked Alexander.

He looked surprised. "Don't you have family here?" he asked as he climbed down.

Maisie shook her head. "Our father is out of the country and our mother's in Newport. Remember?"

Alexander studied Maisie and Felix for a moment. "I've been happy to help you both out," he said. "And happy for the company. But I'm new here, and I have to forge my way alone." He patted his breast pocket. "I have letters of recommendation from Reverend Knox and Mr. Kortright and Mr. Cruger. I can't very well show up on their friends' doorsteps with two children in tow."

"I'm practically thirteen!" Maisie said.

Alexander smiled sympathetically. "Even so," he said, "you two are on your own now."

They watched him hoist his trunk and approach the ticket man.

"Could you direct me to this address?" he asked, holding out a piece of paper.

"Ah!" the man said. "Kortwright and Company. Come and I'll point the way."

Maisie and Felix stood, staring in disbelief as Alexander Hamilton walked around the corner and disappeared from their sight.

For a few minutes, they did not speak or move. Then Maisie turned to her brother, her eyes flashing with anger.

"Who needs Alexander Hamilton?" she said. "We're New Yorkers. We can find Bethune Street without him."

She didn't wait for Felix to answer. Instead, she just started walking north, muttering, "I hate Alexander Hamilton. I *hate* him!"

As usual, Felix ran to catch up with her. The streets grew more crowded with men in powdered wigs and long coats. Felix tried to get his bearings, but nothing looked familiar at all. They passed John Street. Then William Street. The crowds thinned and soon the streets gave way to hills and trees.

"Maisie," Felix said. "What if there isn't a Bethune Street yet?"

She paused.

"There has to be," she said.

But the tone in her voice let him know that she had the same worry as he did. No Bethune Street. No apartment. No Alexander Hamilton. Maybe no way back home.

Maisie stared at the Hudson River, which stretched out in front of her and Felix. She had decided that the best way to find Bethune Street wasn't through the woods that covered what she knew as Chinatown and SoHo, but to walk west and follow the river. Their old apartment was on the corner of Bethune Street and Greenwich Street, two blocks from the Hudson River. If they followed the river north, Maisie felt certain she could figure out where Bethune Street was. Even though their actual apartment building wouldn't be there, it would be exciting to see what was there instead.

The waterfront was busy with sailors and merchants, the harbor lined with ships. But as they headed north, once again the land became hilly and wooded and the crowds vanished.

"Maisie," Felix said, "if there's no Chinatown and no SoHo, I don't think there's going to be a Greenwich Village, either."

He was tired of walking. Unlike the bike paths and walking paths that lined the river when they lived in New York, the banks of the Hudson River in 1772 were muddy and empty. Felix worried that Native Americans might live in these woods, and that they might not be too friendly to trespassers.

"But if we can find where it should be," Maisie said, "then maybe we can travel forward enough years to be back where we want to be."

Felix stopped walking and looked at his sister's desperate face.

"Oh, Maisie," he said, "is that what you've been thinking?"

Maisie nodded. "If we want it bad enough, I think it can work."

"But what about the coin? And what about Alexander Hamilton?"

"I don't know," she admitted.

Slowly, they continued up the bank, climbing over rocks and pushing through ferns and low hanging tree limbs.

Finally Felix said, "I don't want you to be disappointed, but I think we can't go back unless we give that coin to Alexander. If we can find him again."

"What if that coin got us to him, just so he could get us back here? Did you ever think of that?"

"It doesn't make sense—" Felix began.

"Shhh," Maisie said. "I'm counting."

"Counting what?" Felix said.

"Well, twenty blocks is a mile, right?"

"Right," Felix said.

"And it takes twenty minutes to walk twenty blocks, right?"

"I guess."

"So I'm counting how many blocks we would have covered by now so that I can tell when we should head east."

The river curved gently eastward. In the distance, Felix saw a canoe gliding upstream.

Maisie stopped abruptly.

"Impossible!" she said.

She walked back for a bit. Then returned to where Felix still stood. She walked ahead of him. Then again returned to him.

"What now?" he asked her.

Maisie looked like she might start to cry. She was positive they were in the right place. But there were no streets, no buildings. No nothing.

"Bethune Street," she managed to say. "It's underwater."

$

"Landfill," Maisie moaned miserably as they once again followed the Hudson River, this time south, back to where the stagecoach dropped them off. "They must have moved the river at some point and filled it in to make more streets."

Felix didn't reply. Now they had to walk back and try to find Alexander Hamilton, who had no interest in seeing them at all.

Maisie was busy making a new plan. She'd heard Alexander ask for directions to Kortwright and Company. They would go there and find him and beg him to help them . . . here was where her plan faltered. What exactly did they need him to do? Felix was probably right. They had to give him the coin.

Maisie walked even faster. The sooner they found Alexander and gave him the coin, the sooner they would be back in The Treasure Chest to try again.

"Okay," Felix said. "Spill."

"Spill what?"

"I know you've got some plan in mind."

"Not a *plan* really. But I think if we give that coin to Alexander, we'll end up back in The Treasure Chest—"

"And?"

"And then we can try again."

Felix groaned. "Maisie—"

Maisie glared at him. "What?"

"Maybe we should stay home and just work on getting used to how things are now."

"You sound like Mom," she said.

"Well, maybe she's right," Felix said.

"No way! I want to go back to how things used to be. I don't care if you come with me or not. But I want things back to normal."

She didn't wait for him to answer her. She practically ran off toward the tree-lined streets that lay up ahead.

CHAPTER 12

Elizabethtown, New Jersey

Maisie and Felix walked into Kortright and Company's offices late that afternoon.

The coin from The Treasure Chest felt heavy in her pocket and she reached in to touch it like a good luck charm. Then she took a big, deep breath and approached the man who seemed to be in charge. He had a large nose with lots of red spidery lines coming from it, bushy white eyebrows, and tobacco-stained teeth.

"Excuse me," Maisie said in her most polite voice, "I am looking for Alexander Hamilton."

The man's entire face crumpled up. "Who?" he practically bellowed.

Maisie took a step back from his smelly breath.

"Alexander Hamilton?" she said. "A short boy with red hair and blue eyes, carrying around a big trunk?"

"Why would a boy with a trunk come into Kortwright and Company?" the man said and waved her away.

"He was looking for Mr. Kortwright," Maisie added.

The man's face relaxed ever so slightly. "Mr. Lawrence Kortwright?" he asked.

Maisie nodded. "Alexander just arrived at noon from Saint Croix via Boston."

The man studied her for a moment, then shuffled off. Maisie and Felix watched him confer with a tall, distinguished-looking man who kept glancing over at them as he listened carefully. Then he nodded, and together the two men approached them.

"Mr. Lawrence Kortwright," the first man announced.

Mr. Kortwright bowed.

Felix, unsure what to do, bowed back, feeling awkward and silly. Although no one actually commented on their peculiar clothes, he saw how they looked them up and down, confused.

"You are looking for young Mr. Hamilton?" Mr. Kortwright asked. He didn't wait for a reply. "He was in earlier and has taken his leave with Mr. Hercules Mulligan."

"Hercules?" Felix repeated.

"Do you know where Rhinelander's China Shop is? On Water Street?"

Felix shook his head.

"But I'm sure we can find it," Maisie said.

"It's on the edge of the East River wharves," Mr. Kortwright continued.

In Maisie's mind, she imagined the shape of the island of Manhattan, how it came to a point at its tip. They were far enough south to easily reach the East River wharves and to find Water Street and this Hercules Mulligan.

"Thank you," she said.

And then she curtsied, just because she had never had any occasion to curtsy before.

$

In fact, they did find Water Street and Rhinelander's China Shop easily.

"Go ahead," Maisie said as they stood in front of Hercules Mulligan's front door. "Knock."

"Why do I have to knock? You're the one so bent on finding Alexander Hamilton."

"Do you think we can get back home if we don't find him?" Maisie said.

Felix knocked.

They waited for what seemed like forever before Maisie said, "Knock again."

"No one's home," Felix said.

With a sigh, Maisie knocked hard on the door. Still, no one answered, but the door next to it, to Rhinelander's China Shop, flew open and a tall string bean of a man stuck his head out.

"He's not here," the man said. "He's taking around a young man who just arrived from Saint Croix in the Caribbean."

"Do you know where they went?" Maisie asked.

"Probably down the street to Mulligan's Haberdashery."

"Haber what?" Felix asked.

"Haberdashery," the man said. "And a fine one it is, too. No doubt Mulligan is fitting that young man with a suit and a few pairs of britches and shirts. He looked a bit raggedy."

The man squinted at Maisie and Felix.

"You two might benefit from a trip there yourselves," he added.

Felix looked at his knobby knees sticking out beneath his madras shorts. His legs were mud splattered from their walk along the Hudson, and his yellow T-shirt was streaked with dirt. Maisie did not look much better. Her hair was all blond knots and her jeans had a tear at one knee.

"It's an expensive shop, though," the man said thoughtfully. "Gold and silver buttons, lace from France, that sort of thing."

"Maybe we'll just wait here for them," Felix said, sitting on the front steps of Rhinelander's house.

The man nodded and disappeared back into the china shop.

"I guess we look pretty raggedy ourselves," Maisie said in a perfect imitation of the man.

"Haberdashery emergency!" Felix said.

Laughing, Maisie plopped down next to him. "We smell pretty bad, too," she said. "Three weeks on a ship—"

"Don't forget the fire," Felix said.

"A week in a stagecoach—"

"And the walk up the Hudson," Felix added.

They were laughing so hard by this time that they didn't notice the beautiful woman who had come around the corner and now stood watching them with great curiosity.

"Are you children lost?" she asked.

Maisie and Felix stopped mid laugh and looked at her in surprise.

"Oh no," Maisie said quickly. "We're waiting for Mr. Hercules Mulligan."

The woman's back stiffened. She wore a lovely lavender dress with off-white lace trim and tiny pearl buttons. Her chestnut hair was piled high on her head, and she wore white lace gloves on her small hands.

"You know Mr. Mulligan?" she asked.

"Not exactly," Maisie said.

The woman crossed her arms and studied them.

"We came from Saint Croix—"

"Saint Croix!" the woman exclaimed. "Why, you're hurricane children!"

Before they knew what had happened, she had each of them by an arm and practically lifted them in the house.

"Well then," the woman said in a blur of lavender

and lace, "in the bath with both of you."

She led them up a set of stairs and deposited them into separate large bedrooms.

"While I have Birdie heat water for your baths, you may take off those filthy rags," she ordered, closing first one door and then the other firmly.

"Excuse me?" Felix asked.

"Yes?" the woman said.

"Who exactly are you, anyway?"

The woman paused. "Elizabeth Sanders. I'm engaged to marry Hercules."

$

Scrubbed clean and dressed in white cotton nightshirts while their clothes dried, Maisie and Felix sat in the front parlor with Elizabeth Sanders, sipping tea from fine china teacups and waiting for Hercules and Alexander to return.

"So you traveled with this Alexander Hamilton from Saint Croix to meet up with Hercules?" Elizabeth asked, trying to piece together their story.

"Kind of," Maisie said.

Elizabeth said, "Which part is incorrect?"

"Um," Maisie said. "We didn't exactly plan to see Hercules, but then once we were here, well . . ."

Elizabeth waited for her to finish, but Maisie just smiled and sipped her tea.

Thankfully, the front door burst open and Alexander and Hercules emerged laughing and talking like best friends.

"It's just like home," Alexander was saying. "The ships. The crowds. Even the smell!"

Both men laughed heartily at that. But when Alexander saw Maisie and Felix sitting there, he stopped laughing. His violet eyes widened.

"You two?" he said. "How did you find me?"

"Hercules, darling," Elizabeth said, getting to her feet and hurrying to Hercules's side.

Hercules Mulligan was one of the tallest men that Maisie and Felix had ever seen. Six feet six with a wild mane of sandy hair and dressed in a velvet suit with gold buttons and chains gleaming from it.

"They've come from Saint Croix with Mr. Hamilton," Elizabeth said, taking one of Hercules's giant hands in her petite ones.

Hercules turned to Alexander. "You didn't mention companions," he said.

Alexander raised both hands. "Because they aren't. Or rather, they were. They showed up on the island like two water rats and stowed away on the ship with me. I had no choice but to help them. They are only children after all."

"I'm practically thirteen!" Maisie said, jumping to her feet.

"Now, now," Elizabeth said. "The point is they're here, and they're hurricane children. We'll just tuck them in an upstairs bedroom until . . . until . . ."

"Until we can go home," Maisie said.

Alexander glared at her.

Maisie's heart leaped.

$

For the next few days, Maisie and Felix walked around their hometown with Hercules and Alexander. They quickly saw that eighteenth-century Manhattan bore no resemblance to the city where they had grown up. Even worse, the presence of the British mixed with the unhappiness of the colonists made them feel frightened. Fort George, the British army's headquarters, stood high on a hill overlooking all of lower Manhattan. It was impossible to forget that war was coming with Fort George's guns right there pointing down at them.

One evening, Hercules took them to Wall Street

to meet Reverend John Rodgers, who was going to write Alexander a recommendation to the College of New Jersey.

As their carriage moved along Wall Street, Hercules said, "Ah, that Fort George and its battery of guns."

Maisie, looking out the window at the enormous fort on the hill, suddenly said, "Battery? Did you call that a battery?"

"Yes," Hercules said. "The guns form a battery—"

Maisie grinned at Felix. "And that's where the name Battery Park must come from!"

"Battery Park?" Hercules said.

Felix smiled at his sister. Battery Park was a neighborhood that sat at the tip of their Manhattan, probably right where Fort George was now.

"Yeah," Felix said softly. "Battery Park."

"It's hardly a park," Hercules scolded. "Fort George is the headquarters for all the British armies here in the colonies."

The carriage came to a stop, and they all got out. Reverend Rodgers opened the door before they even had a chance to knock, eagerly ushering them inside.

"Come, come," he said cheerfully. "Friends of

Reverend Knox are always welcome in my home."

After he settled them into seats and served them tea, he began to question Alexander about his intentions for studying. All of his sponsors in Saint Croix wanted him to go to the College of New Jersey, and Reverend Rodgers was the man who could get him in.

As the reverend questioned Alexander, Maisie could hardly listen. They talked about Latin and Greek and other subjects that bored her to death. What didn't bore her was to sit and gaze at Alexander, to listen to his deep voice and his easy laugh. She supposed this was what happened when you developed a crush on a boy.

But Felix liked to listen to all the talk about the Sons of Liberty fighting the British on Bowling Green and the Loyalists in the New York Assembly. He liked to hear these men tonight talking about literature and books, too.

"You mean you've had no formal education at all?" Reverend Rodgers was saying. "Even I can't convince the admissions board to accept someone so far behind the others, no matter how brilliant you may be or how many people are recommending you."

"I learn fast, sir," Alexander said. "If I can have a tutor, I'll catch up in no time."

"But a tutor would deplete your college money, son," the reverend said. "No, you'll need to attend a preparatory school. Perhaps on an accelerated track."

"My best friend, Neddy Stevens, is here at King's College," Alexander said. "He told me they have a preparatory school."

Reverend Rodgers snorted. "It takes three years. Why, you can't afford to live in Manhattan for even one year."

"I must go to college," Alexander said.

Reverend Rodgers nodded. "Everyone agrees with you on that point," he said. "There seems to be just one school for you, both academically and financially. Elizabethtown Academy. One of the best schools in the colonies. And perhaps the only one that can get you up to snuff for college."

That quickly, the matter was decided. Everyone was standing and shaking hands.

"Elizabeth's cousins will let you stay with them, I'm sure," Hercules was saying.

"Where are we going?" Maisie asked Alexander.

"*I'm* going to Elizabethtown Academy," he said.

"Yes, but where is that?"

"Across the bay," he answered. "In New Jersey."

Alexander and Hercules walked with Reverend Rodgers back out to the carriage.

Felix looked at Maisie.

"I guess we're moving to New Jersey," he said.

CHAPTER 13

Liberty Hall

"No," Alexander told Maisie and Felix. "Absolutely not."

The three of them stood in the hallway between the bedrooms where they slept on the second floor of Hercules Mulligan's Water Street house.

"But you have to take us with you," Maisie said.

Alexander laughed. "I do not have to do anything of the sort."

They spoke in hushed voices so as not to disturb anyone else in the house.

"If you leave here, Hercules will make us leave, too," Maisie said desperately.

Felix, who had been silent, leaving the pleading to Maisie, had an idea. He held his hand out to

Maisie. "Give me the coin."

She reached into her pocket and pulled out the silver coin.

"Here," she said, giving it not to Felix, but to Alexander.

He didn't take it from her at first. "A coin?" he said suspiciously.

"A silver dollar, to be exact," Maisie told him. "Take it."

Alexander hesitated, but then he accepted the coin from her, holding it up close to his face to examine it. Maisie took Felix's hand, closed her eyes, and waited.

But nothing happened.

She opened her eyes and looked right into Felix's own disappointed ones.

"It didn't work," he said sadly.

"Now what do we do?" Maisie said. She could hear the panic in her own voice. If giving the coin to Alexander Hamilton didn't send them home, then what would?

"I don't understand," Alexander said softly. "This coin is dated 1794." He felt the weight of it in his palm. "It's heavy," he said. "It feels real."

"It is real," Maisie said.

Felix rubbed his temples as if that might help make an idea come to him. "We're missing something," he said.

"Maybe we have to be outside?" Maisie offered.

Felix shook his head. "I don't think that matters."

"Maisie," Alexander asked. "Where did you get this?"

"I can't really explain it," Maisie said.

Puzzled, Alexander handed the coin back to Maisie, who took it from him and put it back in her pocket.

"No," Felix said, "I think he should keep it."

"But it didn't work," Maisie reminded him.

"That's because *we're* not doing something."

Maisie narrowed her eyes at Alexander. "If we let you keep it, can we come to New Jersey with you?" she asked him.

"What you don't seem to understand is that I'm going there as a guest of William Livingston. Do you know what an important man he is?" Alexander asked.

Maisie and Felix both shook their heads.

"How can you have lived on the island of

Manhattan and never heard of William Livingston?" he asked in disbelief. "He's only from the wealthiest family in all of New York."

"Then he won't mind having a couple of more guests, will he?" Maisie said.

"But it's impertinent of me to bring you two along," Alexander said.

From downstairs, the sound of Elizabeth's laughter floated up to them.

"Isn't Elizabeth related to this guy?" Maisie asked.

"Yes," Alexander said.

Maisie smiled. "Fine," she said. "I'll just have to ask her permission to go."

Felix smiled, too. Elizabeth Sanders was kind and, he knew, had a soft spot in her heart for the two raggedy children she'd found on the front steps. He didn't know how they were going to get back to Newport, but he felt pretty confident that Elizabeth Sanders would get them to New Jersey.

$

Maisie and Felix knew of three ways to get to New Jersey from Manhattan: the Lincoln Tunnel, the Holland Tunnel, and the George Washington

Bridge. But in 1772, the only way to get to New Jersey was by ferry. They sailed with a sulking Alexander Hamilton from the wharf just beneath Fort George, across the Hudson River, to Elizabethtown Point. Elizabeth Sanders had said, *Of course my uncle will take you in while you await word from your mother in Rhode Island!* Maisie had hugged Elizabeth in relief.

But Alexander was furious that once again he was stuck with these two children. *It isn't that I don't like you,* he'd explained, *it's that this is the beginning of my new life.*

Now they all stood together at the railing of the ferry, watching first Manhattan Island grow small and disappear from view, then Elizabethtown Point come into sight.

William Livingston had retired as a lawyer and moved his family to New Jersey to live the life of a gentleman farmer. However, Elizabeth Sanders had told Maisie and Felix that her uncle was fiercely opposed to British rule and worked all the time toward the fight for independence. Felix looked forward to nights at Livingston's home, Liberty Hall, listening to more debates about politics like he'd heard on the stagecoach ride from Boston. He was surprised how interesting all of this was. Maybe he was starting to like history, Felix thought.

Livingston's carriage waited for them when they stepped off the ferry. It was a cold November day, with a strong wind howling, and Maisie and Felix were happy to snuggle under a fur blanket inside. They were both wearing clothes from Hercules's Haberdashery: warm wool coats with gold buttons and stiff, white linen shirts. Maisie had on a long, dark red skirt. Felix wore navy blue wool pants that came to just below his knees and thick black stockings. They both wore black boots with silver buckles on them. *This is better than Halloween*, Maisie had whispered after they got dressed. Their own clothes were washed and ironed and folded into a brown paper package tied with string.

Alexander sat across from them, his face pressed to the window as he looked out at the town. Maisie rested her head on Felix's shoulder, happy to be warm and away from the salty air and wind on the ferry. But Felix looked out the window, too, taking in the shingled houses and apple trees.

"It looks a lot like home," Felix said softly,

surprising himself that, for the first time, he had called Rhode Island home.

"Does it?" Alexander said. "It's so different from the islands. From my home," he added.

The carriage came to a stop, and the driver opened its door, announcing "Liberty Hall."

They stepped out, pausing to take in what would be their new home, at least for a while.

The house was big, though not nearly as big as Elm Medona. Fruit trees flanked a walkway that led to the front door, and a few apples still clung to limbs, sending the smell of apple cider through the air.

Felix inhaled deeply. *Funny*, he thought. He had never considered New Jersey the country before.

A man appeared at the front door. Tall and skinny, he grinned out at them.

"Welcome! Welcome to Liberty Hall!"

For the next week, Maisie and Felix got swept up in the social scene at Liberty Hall. Every night there was a dinner party with guests coming from Manhattan or from down the road where other wealthy families had also built houses. After dinner, the Livingston daughters and their friends played the piano for everyone. Then the men retired to the sitting room, where inevitably the discussion turned to the growing tensions between the British and the colonists.

At one of these dinners, Maisie sat across from Alexander. As always, everything around her seemed to disappear as she listened to him speak. He was already attending classes, and he talked about what he was learning and his plans for college as well as his growing allegiance to the colonists. Listening to him, nothing and no one else mattered. Tonight, though, Maisie noticed something that made her sit up straight. Every time Catherine Livingston, who everyone called Miss Kitty, spoke, Alexander's cheeks flushed and his violet eyes grew dreamy.

"Alexander," Maisie said once she noticed this, "I wish I could join the Sons of Liberty."

She said this just to get his attention, of course, but when he didn't look away from Miss Kitty and just made some vague noises toward Maisie, her heart did some weird leaps.

"I would defend the Liberty Pole and fight any Redcoats who tried to blow it up," she said.

The men around her laughed politely.

Miss Kitty turned her large brown eyes on Maisie and said, "How exciting! But not very ladylike."

Maisie fumed. But before she could reply, Miss Kitty had turned her attention back to Alexander, batting her eyes and smiling behind an elaborate silk fan.

$

That night she hardly slept, thinking of Miss Kitty and Alexander. Since she was awake, anyway, she decided to follow him to the cemetery next to Liberty Hall early the next morning. This was how he studied. Pacing and talking to himself early in the morning. She knew he came out here at six o'clock every morning because everyone at dinner always commented on how impressed they were by his dedication and hard work. One night she'd heard noise in the hallway at midnight and peeked out the door of the room she and Felix shared only to find Alexander out there pacing and muttering.

Now here she was watching him pace and talk to himself. There was frost on the grass, and it crackled under Maisie's feet as she made her way to the graveyard.

She waited for a pause in his memorizing before

she stepped out from behind a headstone into his path.

"What brings you here so early?" he asked her, surprised.

Maisie shrugged. Then she blurted, "Homesick, I guess. Couldn't sleep."

"Maisie," Alexander said seriously, "where did you get that coin?"

"Honestly, it belonged to our great-great-grandfather, Phinneas Pickworth." She took it from her pocket. "You should have it, I think."

Alexander accepted the coin, and once again examined it closely.

"Perhaps it was stamped with the wrong date, and that's what makes it collectible?" he said.

Maisie didn't answer.

"I do wonder," Alexander said, holding the coin in his palm, "what will happen if independence is won. Everything will be new. What form of government?" He held the coin out in front of him. "What form of currency?"

He grew thoughtful.

"Strange," he said, looking at her. "I don't miss Saint Croix at all. When I think about it, I have fond feelings. But it's so exciting here. So alive. I believe this is where I'm meant to be."

"I don't know *where* I'm meant to be," Maisie admitted.

"What do you mean?" Alexander asked.

"Well," Maisie said, "I miss Manhattan and living there with my parents. I hate Newport. I really do. And even though my mother's trying hard to make a home for us, nothing feels right."

Alexander nodded. "I understand how being without a parent feels. When my father left, I was devastated. And when my mother died . . ." He looked away from Maisie.

"Even when I go back," Maisie said softly, "everything will be wrong without both of them there."

From behind another headstone, Felix stepped quietly into the early morning light. When he heard Maisie leave, he'd followed her here. He had no idea what she was doing, but now he saw that she just wanted some time alone with Alexander. Felix considered going back to Liberty Hall, and bed, but when he heard her talking about their parents, he wanted to stay. He felt guilty that a part of him had started to adjust to their new situation. Even though he missed their father, Felix was falling into their routine. He couldn't see how fighting it could help anyone.

"Do you know that I have no one?" Alexander said to her. "My father doesn't bother to answer my letters. And my mother died when I was just thirteen." He nudged her gently with his elbow. "Like you almost are," he added.

Felix took a step closer to them, and the frost-covered twigs beneath his feet cracked loudly.

Maisie and Alexander both looked up.

"What are you doing here?" Maisie demanded.

"Just out for a walk?" he said.

She frowned at him.

But Alexander said, "How do you feel, Felix? About the changes in your life?"

"Well," Felix said. "I don't like them. And I miss Dad. But I can't do anything about it."

Alexander nodded. "Yes," he said. "I know."

"Well, you two can be all philosophical," Maisie said, "but I'm mad at them. I'm mad at Mom and Dad for ruining my life!"

"You know, Maisie, that's your choice," Alexander said.

"What? I didn't choose them getting divorced!"

"But you're choosing how you let it affect your life. I could still be working in Cruger's counting house, struggling to make a living on that island. But instead I chose to make an impression, to be someone other than the poor orphan with no future."

Maisie realized Alexander was right. She wanted to ask him more about how he'd managed to overcome all these feelings. Like anger and sadness and frustration.

But instead, she felt herself being lifted up, up, up. The smells of Christmas trees and cinnamon and bread baking surrounded her.

And just like that, she and Felix were standing back in The Treasure Chest.

CHAPTER 14

Great-Aunt Maisie's Orders

"How did that happen?" Maisie said, looking around as if to be sure they really were back.

Felix, just as surprised as his sister, shrugged. "I have no idea."

"I gave him the coin—"

"And then we talked about the divorce and stuff—"

"It doesn't make sense," Maisie said.

Felix agreed. "There's something that happens that we're not figuring out yet. And that something is what brings us back home."

"I wish I had the chance to say good-bye to Alexander," Maisie said sadly.

"Me too," Felix said. "Even though he got mad

at us for following him, I really liked him."

"So did I," Maisie said.

She blushed, but Felix decided not to tease her about it.

"Hey!" he said. "Let's try to find out what he did with that coin."

"How?" Without Internet they couldn't find out anything, Maisie thought for about the millionth time.

"The encyclopedia!" Felix said.

They walked out of The Treasure Chest, being careful to slide the wall back into place. Down the Grand Staircase, past the photograph of young Great-Aunt Maisie and Great-Uncle Thorne, into the Grand Ballroom.

"I think we're done with The Treasure Chest," Maisie said, pausing on the marble floor.

"Agreed," Felix said, relieved.

"I really started to wonder if we would ever get back," Maisie said as they walked through the Dining Room.

"I was worried," Felix admitted. "And unless we figure out how we get back each time, there's a good chance we might really get stuck in the past."

"And what would Mom do without us?" Maisie asked. "Alexander was right. We can't change anything. I guess maybe I have to try to be a little bit nicer."

"You're nice," Felix said softly. "You're just sad."

Maisie turned to her brother. "Yes," she said. "But so are you."

"Well, we have each other," he said.

Maisie and Felix hugged each other good and tight. When they separated, Maisie said, "Who would ever believe that we *time traveled*?"

Felix laughed. "I hardly believe it myself."

$

Back in their apartment, Felix found the F–J encyclopedia and opened it to *H*.

Sure enough, there he was. ALEXANDER HAMILTON.

"You read it," Maisie said.

Felix laughed. "Well, I see why that coin was important," he said. "First secretary of the treasury . . . created the American banking system . . . invented the modern corporation . . . Aide-de-Camp to George Washington—"

"Wow!" Maisie said.

"He graduated from King's College," Felix said, reading more. "Which is today's Columbia University."

"And where his friend Neddy went," Maisie said.

"He really turned into someone important," Felix said, closing the encyclopedia. "His picture's on the ten-dollar bill."

"No way!" Maisie said.

Felix nodded.

"And," he added, grinning at his sister, "he didn't marry Catherine Livingston."

"Really?" Maisie said, delighted. Then she composed herself. "Who cares, anyway? Not me."

"Me neither," Felix said. "Just a small detail."

Maisie smiled. "Thanks, bro," she said.

$

On Sunday, their mother announced that they were going to visit Great-Aunt Maisie and have lunch with her. They stopped at the little bakery on Thames Street that made French *macarons* in pale shades of green and pink and yellow and bought a dozen for her. Great-Aunt Maisie thought that American macaroons, the dense balls of condensed milk and coconut topped with a bright red cherry, were barbaric.

At the Island Retirement Center, they passed through the solarium and into the wing where Great-Aunt Maisie lived.

Ahead of them, they watched a patient dressed in a black-and-white skirt and jacket walking slowly down the hall with the help of a walker. Something about the woman seemed oddly familiar. The fancy suit. The bobbed gray hair.

"Wait a minute!" Maisie shouted. "That's Great-Aunt Maisie!"

At the sound of her name, Great-Aunt Maisie stopped walking and turned around. As usual, she had her face powdered and the two pink spots of rouge on each cheekbone. Her lips wore their usual Chanel Red lipstick. Despite that, something about Great-Aunt Maisie was completely different. Yes, she was actually walking, which Maisie had not seen her do since they'd moved here. But it was more than that. She looked . . . Maisie struggled for the word . . . alive!

"Hello!" Great-Aunt Maisie called to them. She waved one hand like she was a queen.

"Great-Aunt Maisie!" their mother gasped, hurrying toward her. "What on earth do you think you're doing?"

"Going to lunch," Great-Aunt Maisie said. "It's almost noon."

"But . . . but . . . you're walking!" their mother sputtered.

Great-Aunt Maisie looked pleased. "Yes, Jennifer," she said, "I am. Now, would you like to join me for some of the poor excuse for food that they serve here? I believe they have chowder today. New England clam chowder."

With that, she returned to her slow but steady walk down the corridor.

"Go help her," their mother said, nudging first Felix and then Maisie toward their aunt. "I've got to find a nurse."

Maisie and Felix scurried after Great-Aunt Maisie, catching up to her quickly.

"How did you get so much better?" Maisie said.

Great-Aunt Maisie paused. She lifted her eyes until they met Maisie's straight on.

"A very good question, dear," she said.

With that, she continued on.

$

By the time their mother joined them in the dining room, Great-Aunt Maisie had already ordered and sent back one cup of clam chowder because she found it wasn't hot enough. Maisie had a grilled cheese on a plate in front of her and Felix had a hot dog.

"It is New England clam chowder," Great-Aunt Maisie said as soon as their mother sat down, "but it's lukewarm."

Their mother looked completely flustered.

"No one can explain why you were able to get up from your chair yesterday and walk for the first time in six months," she said. "Everyone is baffled."

Great-Aunt Maisie's blue eyes twinkled. "Doctors," she said. "What do they know about anything?"

The waitress appeared with another bowl of chowder and placed it in front of Great-Aunt Maisie.

Great-Aunt Maisie frowned.

"What's wrong now?" the waitress asked.

"Why, it's too hot!"

"How do you know? You haven't tried it yet," the waitress said.

"I can tell. Look at the steam coming from it."

She started to remove the bowl, but Great-Aunt

Maisie shooed her away. "Well, it will cool eventually, won't it?" she said.

After the waitress left, their mother whispered, "You must be nicer to the staff here."

"All I want is a bowl of New England clam chowder that I can eat," Great-Aunt Maisie said.

She took a spoonful and blew on it. The three of them watched her and then looked at one another.

"Your hand is so steady," their mother said.

"Mmmm," Great-Aunt Maisie said.

They watched as she ate that spoonful and another.

"Instead of staring at me, Jennifer, why don't you go and order some lunch?" Great-Aunt Maisie said.

Their mother mumbled, "All right," and went to put in her order.

Great-Aunt Maisie put the spoon down and smiled at Maisie and Felix.

"Well," she said, "how have you two been?"

Maisie blurted, "Oh, Great-Aunt Maisie! We've had the most wonderful adventure!"

"Yes?" she said eagerly.

"We stowed away on a ship," Maisie said.

"And we took a stagecoach from Boston to New York—" Felix added.

"And New York looked so different we could hardly find our way around," Maisie said.

Great-Aunt Maisie clapped her hands in delight.

"Tell me, children, who was it you met?" she asked.

"Alexander Hamilton," Maisie said.

"Oh! That is a good one!" Great-Aunt Maisie said. "Bravo!"

"Great-Aunt Maisie," Felix said, looking around to be sure no one could hear him. "Did you do this, too? You and Thorne?"

At the sound of her brother's name, Great-Aunt Maisie's eyes darkened.

"Thorne," she said. "Don't say his name in my presence. That rascal! That—"

"Are you two upsetting Great-Aunt Maisie?" their mother said, sitting down.

Maisie shook her head.

"They were just telling me about their lovely weekend," Great-Aunt Maisie said. She took another spoonful of chowder. "Oh, dear," she said to their mother, "they forgot to bring me those little oyster crackers I like so much with my chowder.

Would you find some for me?"

"Sure," their mother said, forcing a smile.

As soon as she walked off, Great-Aunt Maisie leaned toward them.

"My guess," Great-Aunt Maisie said in a low voice, "is that he's in London. At least he was last time I heard."

"When was that?" Felix asked.

"1941," Great-Aunt Maisie said.

"That was, like, seventy years ago!" Maisie said.

"Was it?" Great-Aunt Maisie said. "My, time flies."

She closed her eyes, and for a moment they thought she had fallen asleep. But then she murmured, "Alexander Hamilton."

Great-Aunt Maisie opened her eyes again and said with a sigh, "I never got to meet him. I bet he was brilliant."

"Yes, he was," Maisie said.

"Anyone who wrote *The Federalist Papers* would have to be brilliant. And confident—"

"Yes," Maisie agreed.

Great-Aunt Maisie smiled and nodded. "Was he very handsome?"

"He's, like, five seven," Felix said at the exact same time that Maisie gushed, "Oh, very handsome!"

"A small man!" Great-Aunt Maisie said. "Hmm. I actually like a small man."

"Great-Aunt Maisie!" their mother said, appearing at the table with two packages of oyster crackers. "Are you telling them about old boyfriends?"

"Not at all," Great-Aunt Maisie said. "We're discussing Alexander Hamilton."

Their mother thought a moment. "I know he's on money. The ten? The twenty?"

"He was the first secretary of the treasury," Felix said. "That's why."

Their mother looked at them, surprised. "Well, I guess the Anne Hutchinson Elementary School is teaching you quite a bit already."

"Did they have pudding?" Great-Aunt Maisie asked their mother.

Maisie and Felix could tell their mother's patience was running thin.

"Yes," she said evenly.

"Butterscotch?" Great-Aunt Maisie asked.

"Why don't I go check?" their mother said, getting up again.

"When do you think you'll go again?" Great-Aunt Maisie asked as soon as she was out of earshot.

"Oh," Felix said quickly, "we're not going to go again."

"What?" Great-Aunt Maisie said, her back stiffening.

"We almost didn't get back this time," Maisie said. "Alexander kept trying to ditch us, and we had to sleep on a beach and—"

"But you must go back," Great-Aunt Maisie said.

"Really, Great-Aunt Maisie," Maisie said. "We agreed. No more."

Their mother was approaching again with a small dish of butterscotch pudding.

"You don't understand," Great-Aunt Maisie said firmly. "You *must* go back again. You must go to The Treasure Chest and travel in time."

"Butterscotch!" their mother said triumphantly.

Great-Aunt Maisie slowly got to her feet. "I've lost my appetite," she said.

"Let me help you," their mother said, taking her elbow.

But Great-Aunt Maisie wouldn't let her hold on.

"Only the children can help me," she said, leveling her gaze at Maisie and Felix. "You will, won't you, children?"

Felix turned to Maisie. She chewed her bottom lip as she thought. Everyone seemed to be holding their breaths until Maisie nodded.

"Felix?" Great-Aunt Maisie said.

Felix nodded, too.

"Wonderful!" Great-Aunt Maisie said, sitting back down. "I think I will have a taste of this." She dug a spoon into the pudding and took a bite.

Maisie and Felix looked at each other. It seemed they would go back to The Treasure Chest again after all.

Alexander Hamilton

January 11, 1755–July 12, 1804

lexander Hamilton was born on the tiny island of Nevis in the British West Indies. After his mother, Rachel Faucett Lavien, divorced her first husband, she moved to nearby Saint Croix. There she met James Hamilton and had Alexander and his older brother, James. When Alexander's father abandoned the family, his mother opened a small store in Christiansted. Alexander loved books and loved going to school. His mother had a small library filled with the classics of the time, and he read them all at a young age.

In February 1768, a yellow fever epidemic swept Saint Croix, and both Alexander and his mother fell ill. Although Alexander recovered, his mother died, leaving him orphaned. The family of Alexander's friend Neddy Stevens took him in. They also bought his mother's collection of books at an auction of her belongings so that Alexander could have them. At the age of thirteen, Alexander got a job as a clerk at Beekman and Cruger, a large import and export company that had its main office in New York City. New York was one of the thirteen colonies and was still ruled by Britain. Goods shipped to and from Saint Croix avoided the heavy taxes imposed on the colonies by the British. Saint Croix was also very active in the slave trade.

When Alexander was sixteen years old, his boss, Nicholas Cruger, got sick and went home to New York, leaving him in charge of the company for over five months. Local merchants and traders were impressed with how wise and confident Alexander was in this role. He was a tough negotiator and a good businessman. However, when Nicholas Cruger returned, Alexander reluctantly went back to his job as a clerk. He dreamed of joining Neddy, who now lived in New York and was studying at King's College (now Columbia University) to become a physician.

On August 31, 1772, a hurricane hit the island, devastating Christiansted. Alexander had already had some poems published in the newspaper, the *Royal Danish-American Gazette*. But in the aftermath of the hurricane, he wrote an essay describing its effects on Saint Croix. His mentor, Reverend Knox, and other community leaders were so impressed with his writing skills that they created a fund to send him to college in New York. That October, Alexander set sail for America. He never again set foot on Saint Croix.

Alexander lived with the Livingston family in New Jersey while he studied for the tests that would gain him entrance to college. Although he wanted to attend King's College, the Livingston family and others urged him to apply to the College of New Jersey (now known as Princeton University). However, the president there did not like the arrogant young man and declined him admission. King's College accepted him happily, and Alexander became a familiar figure on campus as he strode around memorizing by speaking out loud to himself. At only 5'7", he made an impression on everyone he met because of his keen intelligence and his passion to make a name for himself in the colonies.

When Alexander arrived in New York, tensions between the colonists and the British were building, and the Revolution was near. In 1776, he left college before graduating to fight for freedom. He was an officer in the Continental army and soon became one of General George Washington's most trusted advisers, writing reports and letters for him and going on important military missions.

Alexander believed in a strong central government. After the war, he was sent to the

Continental Congress as a representative from New York. There, and at the Annapolis Convention, he fought that the interests of the union as a whole should be placed over those of the individual states. The only New Yorker to sign the Constitution, he wrote a series of fifty-one essays urging the people of New York to approve the Constitution. These essays, which are still considered the best explanations of the Constitution, became known as *The Federalist Papers*. (*The Federalist Papers* also include essays by John Jay and James Madison.)

In September 1789, Alexander was named the nation's first secretary of the treasury. Some historians consider this the most important of the executive departments because the new government had to find ways to pay off the debt incurred during the Revolutionary War. Alexander and Thomas Jefferson disagreed on many things. For example, Alexander believed that the nation should pay off the individual states' debts; Jefferson believed each state should pay its own debts. The men made a deal: Jefferson would back Alexander's plan if Alexander backed Jefferson's idea to move the nation's capital from New York to land near Virginia.

Before retiring to his home, the Grange, in Manhattan, Alexander established a national bank, helped rebuild the army, introduced the dollar system, and helped to create the silver dollar.

In 1804, Alexander was actively against Aaron Burr's bid for governor of New York. After Burr lost the race, he challenged Alexander to a duel. Although duels were common at the time, Alexander himself had worked to make them illegal in New York after his own son was killed in one. Therefore, Hamilton met Burr on the New Jersey side of the Hudson River at dawn on July 11, 1804. It is believed that Alexander's gun misfired, leading Burr to shoot and mortally wound him. He was carried back to New York City and died the next afternoon.

Known as the Little Lion because of his small stature and great power, Alexander Hamilton is considered one of the Founding Fathers of the United States of America.

I do so much research for each book in The Treasure Chest series and discover so many cool facts that I can't fit into every book. Here are some of my favorites from my research for *The Treasure Chest: #2 Alexander Hamilton: Little Lion*. Enjoy!

Alexander Hamilton is always described as one of the Founding Fathers. But what does that term "Founding Fathers" mean? The phrase was first used by President Warren G. Harding at the Republican National Convention in 1916, when he was a senator. But more famously he used it in his presidential inaugural speech five years later. Many people think that the term Founding Fathers actually refers to the first presidents of the United States. Although they are included in that group, many of the Founding Fathers never became presidents. However, they were all political leaders or statesmen who either signed the Declaration of Independence, fought in the American Revolution, framed the Constitution, or signed the Articles of Confederation. There isn't an actual list of these men (yes, they are all men), so some people consider *anyone* who contributed to creating the United States of America a Founding Father. That means that there are hundreds of Founding Fathers. But there are seven who arguably everyone considers a Founding Father. One is Alexander Hamilton. The other six are:

GEORGE WASHINGTON:

Everyone knows that George Washington was the first president of the new United States of America. He took the oath of office in 1789 when the capital was in New York, not Washington, DC (the move didn't happen until the following year). Perhaps being the first president would have qualified him as a Founding Father, but it was his dedication to creating the United States that secured him that spot. In 1775, Washington was one of the Virginia delegates to the Second Continental Congress. By the time they met in Philadelphia, the American Revolution had begun with the battles of Lexington and Concord. Washington was elected commander in chief of the Continental army. The troops he took command of that summer in

Cambridge, Massachusetts, were ill trained and lacked supplies. But he managed to teach them discipline and strategy during the harsh, six-year war. Although his troops often lost battles and land, they persevered through the cold winter at Valley Forge to go on and win the Battle of Yorktown in 1781. A gentleman farmer, Washington wanted nothing more than to retire to his farm at Mount Vernon. But when he realized that the Articles of Confederation were not providing adequate government, he became influential in calling the Constitutional Convention in Philadelphia in 1787. There, the new Constitution was ratified, and George Washington unanimously was elected president.

THOMAS JEFFERSON:

It is said that Thomas Jefferson contributed his pen rather than his voice to the American Revolution. Called the "silent member" of Congress, Jefferson was the principal author of the Declaration of Independence, written in the summer of 1776 when he was only thirty-three years old. Interestingly, Jefferson and Alexander Hamilton disagreed on many things, so much so that Jefferson resigned as secretary of state in President Washington's cabinet in 1793. Both men believed in the future and strength of the United States, but they had very different opinions on how to obtain that. Jefferson, a passionate farmer, wanted an agrarian society; he believed the nation's strength lay in its agricultural roots. Hamilton believed in an industrial society. Jefferson was opposed to a strong central government authority and believed that the people were the final decision makers. Hamilton supported a strong government that would help industry grow. Yet Hamilton supported Jefferson for president in 1800 when he ran against Aaron Burr, the man who would kill Hamilton in a duel four years later. After two terms as president, Thomas Jefferson retired to Monticello, his home in Virginia, where he died on July 4, 1826, a few hours before John Adams, who died on the very the same day.

JOHN ADAMS:

John Adams was a delegate from Massachusetts to both the First and Second Continental Congresses and is known to have been a leader in persuading Congress to declare independence. It was John

Adams who nominated George Washington to be commander in chief. Not only did he help Jefferson with ideas for the Declaration of Independence, but he was also its main advocate in Congress. Adams was the United States' first vice president, serving two terms under Washington. He became our second president and served for one term before being defeated by Jefferson. The two men had been friends for many years, but political differences when Adams was president caused Adams to become enemies with both Jefferson and Hamilton. His last words were: "Thomas Jefferson survives." But Jefferson had died at Monticello a few hours earlier, on July 4, 1826. John Adams's son, John Quincy Adams, became our sixth president.

JAMES MADISON:

The man who would become our nation's fourth president, James Madison, was a Virginia delegate to the Constitutional Convention in Philadelphia. He quickly became known as one of its most emphatic debaters. With Alexander Hamilton and John Jay, Madison wrote the Federalist Papers, which led to the ratification of the Constitution. Often referred to as the "Father of the Constitution," Madison would protest by saying that the Constitution was not the "off-spring of a single brain, but the work of many heads and many hands." He also helped frame the Bill of Rights, which are the first ten amendments to the Constitution. These amendments were written to help protect liberty and include freedom of speech, press, and religion. His opposition to Alexander Hamilton's proposals to put power in the hands of the wealthy led Madison to form the Jeffersonian party, which later became the Democratic-Republican Party.

BENJAMIN FRANKLIN:

Benjamin Franklin is famous for being an inventor, a writer, a scientist, and a patriot. His inventions include the lightning rod, bifocal glasses, and a stove known as the Franklin stove. The famous story of him flying a kite with an iron key tied to it during a thunderstorm led to his invention of the lightning rod. In that experiment, he learned that metal received the electrical charge while the silk ribbon he held received none. But Franklin was also an inventor of ideas. He started the first free lending library and the first volunteer fire department. As the publisher of *Poor Richard's Almanack*, Franklin wrote many adages and pieces of wisdom that are still used today, such as "A penny saved is a penny earned." The circulation of *Poor Richard's Almanack* was about ten thousand copies a year, which is equal to three million copies in modern times. But none of these accomplishments are what earned Benjamin Franklin the title of "The First American." That was bestowed on him for his relentless support of the birth of our nation. Franklin was part of the Committee of Five, who drafted the Declaration of Independence. Later, as the ambassador to France, Franklin worked tirelessly to represent the United States and to secure France as a military ally. When he returned from France, he was named as the first postmaster general of the United States. Benjamin Franklin is the only Founding Father who signed all four of the major documents of the founding of the United States: the Declaration of Independence, the Treaty of Paris, the Treaty of Alliance with France, and the Constitution. He is often called the only president of the United States who was never president of the United States. Since 1914, his portrait has been on our one-hundred-dollar bills.

JOHN JAY:

Along with Alexander Hamilton and James Madison, John Jay was an author of the Federalist Papers, which argued for ratification of the Constitution. Born in New York, Jay was an extraordinary student, graduating from King's College (now Columbia University) at the age of eighteen. John Jay married Sarah Livingston, the daughter of William Livingston, the governor of New Jersey. It was the Livingstons who Alexander Hamilton lived with when he first came to the colonies. Jay was the second-youngest delegate at the First Continental Congress. He was twenty-eight; Edward Rutledge of South Carolina was twenty-five and became the youngest signer of the Declaration of Independence, which Jay refused to sign. Although John Jay is one of our Founding Fathers, he initially opposed independence from Great Britain. Jay was known for his moderate course during this highly charged political time. In the months before the Declaration of Independence, Jay worked on efforts to make peace with Great Britain, and was on the committee that wrote the Olive Branch Petition during the Second Continental Congress. In the time immediately afterward, Jay returned to New York where he worked on drafting the state's constitution and ultimately served as the first chief justice of the New York State Supreme Court. However, he was swept back into national politics in 1779 when he was selected to serve as ambassador to Spain. Later he was sent to Paris as part of the American delegation negotiating the peace terms that ended America's War of Independence with Britain, resulting in the signing of the Treaty of Paris. In 1789, George Washington named him the first chief justice of the United States' newly founded Supreme Court.

Continue your adventures in *The Treasure Chest No. 3 Pearl Buck: Jewel of the East*!

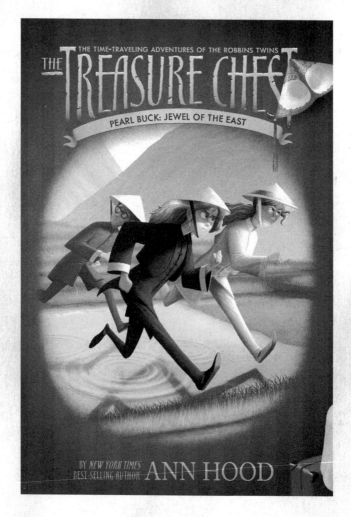

Maisie and Felix landed with a thud.

Where are we now? Maisie wondered as she struggled to get her bearings. It was dark and smelled like the produce stand at the natural-food market. She pushed her arms upward and struggled to the surface, moving the small, hard grains that surrounded her out of the way as she did. Was she in a sandpit? When her head popped out she came face-to-face with an old, wizened Chinese man. His face was weathered and deeply wrinkled, and his wispy, white hair was tied back in a pigtail.

The old man began to shout at her in Chinese, waving his arms and jumping up and down.

Maisie looked down. She had landed, she realized, in a giant basket of rice. That basket of rice stood next to many more baskets of rice, which stood in a row of small stalls selling vegetables. From her perch, Maisie could see green beans and radishes and green cabbages. What she didn't see was Felix.

Still shouting at her, the old man took her arm and pulled hard. Maisie tumbled from the basket in a shower of rice.

"I'm sorry," she said, getting to her feet and

wiping dirt from her chocolate-brown party skirt.

The old man practically picked her up by the nape of her neck and carried her like a kitten through the crowded marketplace, Maisie's legs kicking the air in protest. He kept screaming at her until they reached the end of the market, where he deposited her harshly on the ground.

Maisie sat a moment, rubbing the back of her neck where he'd held on to her. In front of her was a riverbank and a muddy river with boats moving slowly along it. Some of the boats had white sails, others were painted bright colors. She smiled. They had come all the way to China! A surge of excitement coursed through her as she looked around. Men and women passed, wearing cotton tunics and pants and triangular straw hats carrying small baskets of food. They stared openly at Maisie, whispering to one another in Chinese.

China!

Slowly, Maisie got to her feet and went back into the marketplace. *Felix has to be in here somewhere. Doesn't he?* she wondered. Stalls lined both sides, and people haggled over prices in loud Chinese. The first stalls had piles of live crabs and high heaps of small silver fish and piles of ugly, flat fish. Next came stalls that sold glistening, brown ducks cooking on spits over coals, their long necks tucked against their wings. Maisie paused over the mountains of chilies—red, green, yellow, skinny, fat, round, long—and then at the baskets of spices. Cinnamon sticks and whole peppercorns, gnarly ginger root and clusters of purple garlic.

At the vegetable stalls, Maisie crossed to the other side of the market to avoid the old man whose rice she had landed in. Although she could recognize most of what she saw, she stopped and picked up a long, squash-type thing with a reddish-brown skin. The woman who ran the stall slapped Maisie's hand and took the vegetable from her, speaking rapid Chinese to her.

"Sorry," Maisie said again. Would she spend her whole time here apologizing?

The woman pointed to a row of the vegetables. She lifted one, pointing to the white interior dotted with holes. It looked like lace. Maisie understood that the woman was trying to convince her of its freshness.

Maisie nodded politely, then moved on, past red

peppers and melons in all sizes and shapes and colors.

"Were you even going to try to find me?" Felix said from behind her.

"We're in China!" she said with delight.

THE TREASURE CHEST

DON'T MISS ANY OF THESE ADVENTURES!

Nº. 1 Clara Barton: Angel of the Battlefield
The Woman Who Founded the American Red Cross

Nº. 2 Alexander Hamilton: Little Lion
The First United States Secretary of the Treasury

Nº. 3 Pearl Buck: Jewel of the East
The Nobel Prize–winning Writer

Nº. 4 Harry Houdini: Prince of Air
The World's Greatest Escape Artist

Nº. 5 Crazy Horse: Brave Warrior
The War Leader of the Oglala Lakota

Nº. 6 Queen Liliuokalani: Royal Prisoner
The Last Queen of Hawaii

www.treasurechestseries.com